icope

**ADVANCE PRAISE FOR
ANDREW DUNCAN WORTHINGTON'S**

WALLS

This is the debut of a major new talent. Straightforwardly brilliant writing. This book is so honest, so American, so true to what it is like to be young in America today. At moments, Worthington reminds me of Fitzgerald, at other times of Salinger, and then, at other times, of Beckett. One more big name: If Knut Hamsun were a young American writing *Hunger* today, this is the book he would write. The subjectivity of the contemporary experience of our crazy, drug, text and PlayStation-fueled culture is perfectly described. If Worthington can continue to write as well as he does in this novel, he will be one of the greats of the start of the twenty-first century.

--Clancy Martin, author of *How to Sell*

Andrew Duncan Worthington's debut novel, *Walls,* is a book about jobs and boredom, Playstation and needing to poop, daydreaming and girls, planes that never leave the tarmac and Ohio. This book will make you feel like you're stranded in Ohio and you can't get away. Of course, it might be that you don't want to leave. It has a strong attraction, a strong pull. *Walls* is a strong-ass book.

--Scott McClanahan, author of *Hill William*

Noah Cicero, Jordan Castro, Andrew Worthington, me: What do we have in common? We're all from Ohio. We all smoke cigarettes; one of us has the outline of Ohio tattooed on our neck. Rt. 8, Applebee's, the Browns, Bud Light, Coors Light, hallucinogens, throwing snowballs at trains while high on shrooms, Best Buy, Target, Marlboro Reds, Camel Blues, the Cuyahoga… this is a novel about Ohio, and to a lesser extent, Taco Bell. Also NYC and Kent State and mental hospitals and CNN and Iraq… if you're not sold by now: fuck you.

--Elizabeth Ellen, author of *Fast Machine*

WALLS

ANDREW
DUNCAN
WORTHINGTON

Copyright © 2014 Andrew Duncan Worthington
All rights reserved.
CCM Design by *Michael J Seidlinger*
ISBN - 978-1-937865-28-3

For more information, find CCM at:

http://copingmechanisms.net

This is a work of fiction. Any resemblance to real life is purely coincidental.

Table of Contents

An Eyesore ……………………....11
The Julia Page ……........................37
On Top …………….......................57
Walls …………….........................81
Different Size Beds ………...........133
Indiana Jones #4 ……………......159
Come Back Whenever ……….…..181

AN EYESORE
•

"The structure is forty-nine stories high, and most days no one occupies it. It is a fifty-seven yard wide cylinder with a burnt beige hue. At the bottom, facing towards Old Route 8, there is a door-like outline that is half a dozen stories tall, but it is not the door. There is a door but it is an everyday office-building door, unnoticeable to the eyes of an automobile passing by. The top does not appear to be flat. It forms a crown, or at least that is one possibility that the prickly shadows spiking out of it suggest. It is located at the corner of Old Route 8 and Portage Trail. The trail extends east to west throughout the county. It gets its name from the indigenous folks who used to occupy the Cuyahoga River Valley. 'To portage' is to carry a sea vessel between two bodies of water. The Indians would carry their canoes between the Cuyahoga and Tuscarawas rivers. 'Portage' is the translation the European invaders chose. It isn't the word the Indians would have used. Old Route 8 used to be the main thruway for automobile traffic between Cleveland and Canton. The structure now residing at this corner can be seen for several miles along Old Route 8. Its gaze reaches just further than the entire twenty-four and a half mile stretch of Portage Trail.

"By the turn of the millennium, there were only vague memories of this structure's origins. It was built during the sixties. It was meant to be the beginning of a commercial focal point for the county. The plans allegedly called for a restaurant to be near the top floor, and a television station would also have been based near the top of the structure, although one can imagine that the six-o'clock news still would have featured a forged city skyline back drop behind its anchors, because this structure is forty stories higher than any other building within over 50 miles, and it is well-known within media marketing departments that television audiences prefer to live under the semi-conscious illusion that their airwaves come straight from the center of the metropolis, where all information is simultaneously generated and transmitted.

"It has been rumored that the project failed due to the inability of its owner to find tenants for the thirty or so floors below the top. The economy of the surrounding area did not contain enough businesses to fill the building. Saltbox-, Cape Cod-, and Colonial-style houses, inhabited mostly by one or two families, fill most of the surrounding town, which technically is an incorporated city, with a population of about 50,000. Along Old Route 8 there is also subsidized government housing that lines one side of its four-lane highway. Spilling over from the adjacent city of Akron, such residents lacked the funds necessary for the high rents the owner of the tall structure was seeking. Meanwhile, any young, cosmopolitan professionals from the Akron area, who would have had the necessary funds, were disinclined from residing there due to the proximity of the subsidized government housing.

"A local television station, the WB, now owns at least part of the uninhabited building, using it to send frequencies to the surrounding communities. Some say that mobile phone companies pay rent for similar purposes. This application of the structure's height does not at all utilize its interior and architectural depth—a normal electric transmission tower would suffice—and so it is commonly agreed that the original owner must have lost a great sum of money from its construction.

"Here it is up ahead on your right, even though we are still half a dozen miles away. Those of you on the left-hand side of the bus may not be able to see it yet, but you will soon enough. Those of you on the right can of course al[...] will be approaching Old Route 8 in the next few minutes, at which point all of you will see it clearly. Again, I apologize that the owners have not yet granted permission for a tour of the building—I haven't even been in it—but you will be able to get close to it from the bottom.

"Now, as we approach Old 8, I have to ask that you all return to fully secure positions in your seats with your seat belts on. You may not be familiar with the term "inertia"—it means that an object in motion stays in motion. We will be stopping at more and more lights as we get nearer to the center of town. There are 52 bodies—54 including our driver, Dave, and me. Your 52 bodies will indeed stay in motion even as he pushes the brakes at the stoplights and stop signs. That is why I must ask that you buckle up to avoid smashing open your skull on the seat in front of you.

"You all should now be able to see it almost in its entirety. Up here to the left across the corner is a British Petroleum gas station. The owners of BP bought that corner lot thirty-two years ago for just less than a million dollars, while a typical lot of that size in this city most likely wouldn't cost more than 100,000 U.S. dollars. It was a big story in the local papers, because the original owners of the lot had refused all offers for the land. I believe they said it had sentimental value to them. They had grown up there. Their father had grown up there. Regardless, they gave in once BP offered a high enough price.

"We are now pulling into the lot of the building itself. In front of it, by the old highway, is The Cathedral of Resurrected Angels, headed by the minister Marvin Eisley. You may have seen him on television at some point—they broadcast all of his sermons on the WB and its sister networks.

"Anywhere over there is fine, Dave.

"So across the lot is the Cathedral Buffet, where many of the members of the church go for brunch after the Sunday events. Okay, here we are. I have to ask that you exit the bus calmly and with respect for your fellow passengers. First row first, then the second, the third, and so on. You can approach the building as you wish, but I do have to ask that you not encroach within ten feet of the structure itself. After you have all had a good look, you are free to get lunch. There are several dining establishments just to the south of this lot, along this side of the highway. Any questions? Okay, then. Let's plan to meet back here in an hour."

Mom and Dad were waving as I exited the gate. They noticed me before I noticed them. They walked towards me, Mom in front of Dad. I gave part-smile, part-wave.

"Hi Tom!"

"Hi."

I hugged her.

"Tom."

"Hey."

I nodded at him. He nodded at me.

We began walking towards the luggage pick-up.

"Did you bring a suitcase?" asked Mom.

"No, just this," I said. I shrugged the straps on my backpack.

"We're parked over here, anyways," said Dad.

It was 10:15. All seven of the airlines' ticket counters were closed as we passed. A janitor was sweeping the carpet at the other end of the corridor. I wondered if my flight was the last to come into the airport that day.

"How was your flight?" asked Mom.

"Good," I said. "It just left a little late."

There were several hundred cars in the lot, most of them overnight or long-term parking. As we approached Dad's car, he opened the trunk with a remote on his key chain.

"I can just hold this with me," I said.

"Ah, put it in the trunk," he said. "You might as well."

Mom opened the back door.

"I can sit in the back," I said.

"No, you sit up front," she said.

"Alright."

Only three or four cars were visible as we started northbound on Route 8. Near the airport there were mostly just fields and marsh, which I couldn't see, but I knew. As we got further away houses and lights and businesses increased. When we passed a town, four more cars merged into the lanes. Several towns later there were 20 or 30 cars around us. It seemed like what future humans might watch on the Discovery Channel or History Channel. Dad talked about the Cleveland Browns. I started to zone out.

"Tom?"

I hadn't realized Mom was talking to me.

"Sorry," I said. "What'd you ask?"

"I asked if you wanted to pick up some food on the way home."

"No, I'm fine. I picked up some dinner at LaGuardia."

"How are your roommates?" she asked.

"They're good," I said. I tried to think of something

else to say.

"I don't really talk to them that much," I added.

"What do they do?" asked Dad.

"I don't really know exactly," I said. "I think one works at a restaurant and one does something at a law firm. He's like a paralegal or something."

"Do you still like your job at the transportation department?" asked Mom.

"I mean, as much as I ever did. It's okay. Boring but okay."

"So you like New York?" asked Dad.

"Yeah. The city wears me down but I like it most of the time. My job is okay."

"Sounds like a lot of jobs," he said.

"Do you feel like that about your job?" I asked.

"No," he said. "But I do go through phases. It's cyclical."

"When are you guys planning to retire, anyways?" I asked.

Dad grunted. "Probably not for another ten or twelve years, at least," he said. "It depends on the future of the medical industry for me, and for your mom it mainly just depends on her office, if they stay in business, that kind of thing. Isn't that right, Mary?"

"Yeah, I think so."

"Why don't you guys want to retire earlier?"

"Well, for one, I don't know what else I would do," said Dad.

"You could play a lot of golf and make a lot of miniatures and watch movies," I said.

"Yeah, but I'm not going to want to do that stuff all the time. It's nice to have something," he said. "Plus, we lost a lot in this recession."

"Really?" I asked. "Through your investments?"

"Yes," he said. "Through our investments."

I nodded.

"That's what people don't understand, though," he said. "You have to be in it for the long haul, because it's always dipping and rising."

I nodded.

"Take Mr. Eischen, for example, he's a good guy, I guess, but he keeps complaining to me about how he lost in the recession. And I keep telling him: 'Tim, you knew this could happen.'"

I nodded.

"It's like how these people, they complain about Social Security, how it's dying, how they're not getting enough from it in retirement. It's unbelievable. I mean, Social Security is not supposed to be your sole retirement fund. You have to have other savings and investments."

"What do you think of this whole privatization thing?" I asked.

"I think it's a great idea," he said. "I'd do it. The federal government is just playing our taxes on games of chance, the same as we would be doing anyways. Hell, I'd like to do it myself."

"Do you guys think you'll live around here when you retire?" I asked.

"I don't know," said Dad. His lips curved down for a second.

"Yeah, that's a long way away, Tom," said Mom.

More cars entered the highway as we passed through Akron. Dad slowed down to let a car merge.

"C'mon," he said to the car. "I'm letting you on. Now go. Go."

The car sped up. It crossed into the passing lanes. I lost it ahead of us among the tail lights.

We drove past First Street. There was a festival.

"What festival is that? Just 'Rockin' the First'?"

"Who knows," said Dad. "They have festivals all the time."

"Do you guys ever go to them?"

"No, not really," he said.

"We go during the day sometimes, to get elephant ears, maybe," said Mom, "But there's too much trash down there."

We passed 16th Street, 17th Street, 18th Street, 19th Street. I looked down 20th Street. One of my best friends growing up lived down there. I hadn't seen him in a year or two. There was a red light when we got to Old Route 8. When it turned green we drove a few more blocks until Dad turned right onto 28th Street. He turned into our driveway on the corner at the end of the block.

When we got inside, I took my backpack upstairs to my room, which looked how it had always looked, except cleaner. I went downstairs and told them I was going to bed. They said they were going to bed too.

Upstairs I plugged my laptop into the wall behind my dresser. The blind was down over the window near my bed. I pulled it up and looked outside as I waited for the Internet to load. No one was outside. After a few minutes, a car came down the hill. As it continued west into the Valley I couldn't see its tail lights, but I could hear its hum.

I met Sock for drinks. For lack of a better venue we went to the Applebee's near the mall. We each had three draft beers: Coors Light for him and Bud Light for me. After we ordered our first drink I asked him how much his was and he said three dollars. Mine had cost four. I wanted to save the extra dollar and switch beers on my next drink, but I didn't feel like asking the bartender and having a conversation with him, even a small one, and I also didn't want to show a lack of commitment in my choice, so I just got the same the next two. Two extra.

The Browns were playing an exhibition game against the Packers. We talked about how it was nice that they were winning.

"But didn't they win a bunch of preseason games last year?" I asked. "And then they got their asses kicked during the regular season. They only won two games or something, didn't they?"

"Yeah, but they had a lot of injuries."

"They've sucked forever," I said.

"They made it to the playoffs a few years ago, almost," he said.

"I remember that. They made it a few years before that but got their asses kicked in the first round. Didn't they have a pretty good record, too, that last time they almost made it?"

"Yeah, they got screw—well, I guess they didn't get screwed but they almost made it."

"Yeah, the coin toss or whatever to determine tiebreakers for playoff seeds."

"Yeah."

He was looking at the television across from him, above and between two of the tables. I was looking at the television behind the bartender, in front of the kitchen. It was the first time we had seen each other in two years. We didn't have anything in common to talk about except for the Browns. I didn't even really care about the Browns anymore. I glanced over at him, and he looked down at his drink, picked it up, took a sip. He returned his gaze to the screen. I often feel violently angry when people are not able to communicate effectively with me, but, at that moment, I didn't. I took a sip of my drink.

"I have come to the point of conceding it could be decades before they win a Super Bowl," I said.

"Yeah, me too," he said.

After we had finished our third beer we paid the bill. Outside I lit a cigarette and we sat down on a bench in the parking lot facing towards the Best Buy and Target across the street.

"What are you home for, anyways?" he asked.

"A dentist appointment," I said.

He nodded without any other visible reaction, except maybe a blink.

"What's that place over there?" I said. I pointed to the right of Target.

"Oh that used to be McGuiness Bar. Now it's called H & H. Hootie and Hannah's."

"Weird," I said.

I didn't really think it was that weird.

"Supposedly the waitresses are hot and wear, like, no clothes."

"Yeah?"

"That's what Sean said."

"Damn."

"Yeah."

"You want to go there?"

"Sure, I'm down."

We got in his car and drove across the street to another parking lot in front of Hootie and Hannah's.

As he pulled into a spot I said, "Fuck this," and giggled. I wanted to go in, but didn't want to act like I did. We sat in his car staring through the windows. Not many people were inside.

"Yeah, I don't know," he said.

"What—you don't want to go in?" I asked. I didn't really care if we went in but I was starting to have fun.

"No, I don't think so," he said. "Why, do you care?"

"No, not really."

He pulled out of the parking lot. When we got near my parent's house I asked if we could stop at the gas station for cigarettes. He said okay. When he parked I got out of the car. He got out too and followed me into the store. It kind of annoyed me because he didn't smoke and never had, but I figured he was going to pick up something else for himself, but instead he just stood by the counter with me as I bought two cartons of cigarettes. One was Marlboro Reds for me and the other was Camel Blues for a friend back in New York. The cigarette tax in the city had been killing me. I said thanks to the cashier, and Sock led the way back to his car. I bought cigarettes that night because I hadn't wanted to go get them during the day when my parents were awake. They knew that I smoked, but if they saw me walk in the door with two cartons of cigarettes, I would probably have to listen to Mom nag me about it in a caring and concerned way constantly.

But when we pulled into the driveway I saw that the lights were on in the house. Their bedroom light was on, the upstairs bathroom light was on, the living room lights were on, and the kitchen light was on. It was almost midnight.

"Fuck," I said. "They're awake."

Sock didn't say anything.

"Fuck."

"You can leave them in here. We can get lunch tomorrow at Taco Bell, like old times."

I agreed.

So there I was the next day, in front of the Taco Bell with my turn signal on, waiting for oncoming traffic to pass. To the right was a small building lined with different stores. JD Comics and Time Traveler Laser Discs (it kept the name even after the defunction of laser discs) were both still there. The porno shop was still there. The liquor store was still there. Behind them, entire blocks, which used to contain the Route 8 Shopping Center, were demolished. I stared at a dumpster truck that was sitting in the middle of mounds of dirt and garbage. I heard honking and realized it was from a car behind me. There wasn't any oncoming traffic. I had just been sitting there staring. I turned into Taco Bell.

Sock wasn't there yet so I stood in front smoking a cigarette. There was a bus stop by the road. A few people were standing under the awning, looking up at the gray sky that was starting to drizzle, then down the road to see if the bus was coming, then up again, then down the road again. I thought about how shitty it must be to have to ride the bus. The buses didn't come very often and there weren't many stops along the routes.

As I was finishing my cigarette, Sock pulled up in his car, nodding at me, me nodding at him. I said what's up. He said what's up. We walked inside. He told me I could order first. I got a steak quesadilla and two hard tacos supreme. He ordered a bunch of different types of tacos. We each drank water. At one of the tables next to us there was an old lady with her Sunday church hairdo. She was sitting with a middle-aged man who must have been her son. At another table close to us there was a family with parents and kids, all in ragged clothes.

"Do you think they'll ever put anything in there?" I asked Sock, motioning my head towards the vacant lots across the street.

"Who knows," he said.

"Yeah."

"I have a feeling they will have a hard time getting stores to move in. This area sucks."

"Oh yeah, you're a Construction Management major. I forgot," I said. I had just graduated that spring with a degree in political science.

"You're, like, an expert, right? "

"Well, not really, I mean, kind of," he said.

"Where do you want to work when you graduate?"

"Probably in Columbus or Cleveland. Wherever I can get paid."

I nodded.

"I might end up moving out of Ohio," he said.

"Why?"

"Because all the bigger construction projects are other places."

"Yeah, I guess people leave Ohio when they get to our age. No one moves to Ohio, I don't think."

"No, they don't."

There was a thunder outside. The rain began falling down harder.

"Did you go to church with your mom today?" I asked.

He laughed.

"Did you?" he asked.

"No. I don't think either of my parents went, actually. I was asleep, anyways."

"I think my mom doesn't really care for the new ministers they've been bringing in."

"Aren't they kind of fat, two of them?"

"Yeah, I think so."

"And the one who isn't the youth minister, the other one, he's pretty weird. He has a really high voice."

"I pretty much only go on Christmas Eve, nowadays."

"Same here," I said.

We each took sips of our drink.

"I was talking to my friend Jim, you remember him from high school? We played in bands together."

"Yeah."

"I asked him if he still went to mass sometimes with his mom on Sundays and he said yes, and I said I bet it was out of a feeling of guilt, and he said 'Yes. How did you know?'"

"Yeah, a lot of the Catholic people I know who are our age generally are kind of like that, in one way or another."

"But when he was in high school he would only go every once in a while with his mom, and we went all the time to choir and youth group and all that crap. And now we don't go but he still goes every once in a while with his mom."

Sock grunted.

"I don't know," I said. "I think Catholics are more into guilt and tradition. Nothing ever changes. Protestants are more into assimilation and boredom. I don't know what I'm talking about."

"I might know what you're saying."

"Yeah. Oh well."

I put my empty taco wrappers in a trashcan. I took a sip of water from my straw, and it made a gurgling.

"Shall we?" I asked.

"Sure."

We went outside. I got my cigarettes out of his car.

"Anyways, you should come visit me in New York."

"Yeah, I will. I just need to find a date that works."

"Cool. I'll talk to you soon. Let you know the next time I'm in town, too."

"Alright, sounds good."

He got in his car and I walked over to my car with

the cigarettes. The rain was letting up. As he pulled out of the parking lot he hit a pothole and water splashed on the people who were still waiting at the bus stop.

"The thing is, what they did to Nixon is kind of like what they're doing to this coach, I think. The team has been severely penalized, he has been fired, and yet some of these people still want more blood."

"A lot of people?" I asked.

"Yeah, some of them."

"You guys thought it was a pretty good movie, though?"

"Yeah," said Mom. "Another good one. Two for two."

"I thought back then that Frost was a pretty weak opponent for Nixon," said Dad, as he tore a piece of chicken from a kabob and cut it in half.

I looked down at the table, rubbing an onion slice in the hot sauce on my plate. I knew I should just end the conversation, or at least change it. But somehow I was inclined to just beat it to the ground. I chewed the onion. I gulped.

"I don't know," I said. "I think he was supposed to be an underdog and the surprise was that he pulled it off. I think the movie was just supposed to be portraying the American dream, for Frost. He was risking all his money and reputation on the interview. I don't know."

"Eh, how hard could it have been, though, to get Nixon to apologize? The guy's crimes were all there."

"I think they had to get new information and ways of framing it all, in order to get him to do it, in order to get him to admit his wrong-doing rather than just admitting that it happened."

"Eh, that makes sense, I guess. But I remember thinking the guy was a lightweight, pretty much. The movie itself was kind of biased, too. Nixon couldn't have been that hard to crack, and the guy played by Kevin Bacon was made out to be a total villain, essentially."

The kabobs had chicken, onions, peppers, and mushrooms. I wasn't eating the peppers or mushrooms. Marty, the man who lived across the street from our solarium, was working in his garage.

"Do you guys know what Marty does these days?" I asked.

"He sure is an odd one," said Mom.

"Yeah, who knows," said Dad.

We each stared at his property a few moments before returning our concentration to our food. I thought about the two movies we had watched that afternoon. I had picked them up from the library. I had to pay a two dollar and five cent fine that was still on my account from three or four years before.

"Who lives in that house next to Marty?" I asked.

"His name's Neil, I think," said Dad. "He lives by himself. I think he has a daughter who's in grade school but she only seems to visit him every few months, wouldn't you say?"

"Yeah, I don't know the last time I saw her," said Mom.

"And he doesn't take care of the house," said Dad. "The paint is all chipping away, there's weeds growing everywhere, he never cuts the grass."

"Gregg doesn't mow his lawn or rake the leaves often enough either," said Mom. "He never shovels the sidewalk in the winter."

"I mean, does it matter that much?" I asked.

"Yes," said Dad. "It's driving down the property values."

"It's not nearly as bad as some of the houses where I live in New York."

"Well, this isn't New York," said Dad.

I looked at my plate. I scooped some scraps into my mouth.

"Anyone hungry for some pie?" asked Mom. "There's banana cream pie in the fridge."

"I'm fine for now," said Dad. "Maybe later."

"Yeah, I'm full," I said. "But I'll have some later."

"Okay, just let me know, and I'll get it ready."

"What do you guys want to do tonight?" I asked.

"Whatever you want," said Mom.

"Yeah, it's up to you."

"I'm gonna go lie down for a few minutes, and then maybe we can watch something later, or play a game?"

"Yeah, that'd be nice," said Mom.

"Sounds good," said Dad. "I think your sister is going to be calling here sometime soon, right?"

"Yeah, I think she said she would once she got off work," said Mom.

We got out of our seats and carried our dishes to the kitchen.

"Do you need help cleaning them?" I asked Mom.

"No, you go relax," she said. "It's your vacation."

I sat on my bed against my pillow and fell asleep. When I woke up several hours later I walked downstairs. Dad was watching a show on the History Channel about Alger Hiss. Mom was sitting in a chair, reclined and snoring with a Reader's Digest face down on her lap.

"Do you guys want to play a game?" I asked.

"Yeah," said Mom, waking up. "Dad?"

"Yeah, okay."

"What game do you guys want to play?" I asked.

"I'd play Skip-Bo," she said.

Dad nodded. We went into the solarium.

"What did Rachel have to say?" I asked. Dad was shuffling the cards.

"She's busy," said Dad.

"Yeah," said Mom. "She says the hospital has her working till 8 or 9 every day."

Dad dealt us each five cards. We began playing. I was beating Mom, and probably also beating Dad.

"Oh, hell," said Mom.

"Whose turn is it?" asked Dad.

"Hold on," said Mom.

I won two hands later.

"One more game?" asked Mom.

"I'm done," said Dad. "But you guys can go ahead."

"I think I'm going to go to bed," I said.

"Alright," she said. "Do you want to be woken up in the morning?"

"Yeah, I guess. Can you wake me up at ten?"

"I sure can."

"Thanks. Goodnight."

"Goodnight," said Mom. "We love you."

"Goodnight, Tom," said Dad. "It's been good having you home."

I went up to my room. I sat on my bed listening to rap music. I started reading the Wikipedia page for Spinoza. I got distracted with Facebook. I kept looking at photos of my friends. I tried to return my attention to the biography, but I was tired, and lazy, and the effort of moving the mouse and clicking the tab and reading it seemed too great to draw me away from gazing at people I hardly knew getting drunk and posing for photos.

―――――――

The section about Spinoza's upbringing in Holland was on

my screen when I woke up. I clicked on Facebook. I saw Chelsea was online. I had gone on some dates with her a few years before. Her profile said she was engaged. I already knew this. I had looked at her profile twice in the past month. The guy had a mechanical smile, a cross around his neck, and Old Navy apparel. Just like her. I clicked on her icon and began typing:

12:24
ME: Hey Chelsea, congratulations on your marriage!

12:26
Chelsea: Hey!
Thanks!
We're just engaged though, lol
But we did set the date!

12:27
ME: nice
when
?

12:47
CHELSEA: Next year.
March 31.
How are you?

ME: good. still in nyc
visiting home now though
back home

CHELSEA: Oh my gosh
That makes me so jealous.

I always wanted to live in NY.
12:49
What do you do?

ME: i work for the government
the city
department of transporation

CHELSEA: Thats great.

12:50
ME: where are you living?

CHELSEA: I just bought a house in Fairlawn.

ME: Nice
that's like a west Akron suburb, right?

12:52
CHELSEA: Yep.

12:53
ME: whats your job

CHELSEA: I work as an accountant.

12:54
ME: nice

12:59
CHELSEA: Anyways, it was great catching up! Hope all goes well with NYC!

1:02
ME: cool
Chat cannot be sent while Chelsea is offline. You can send it as a Message and she will read them in her Inbox.

ME: later
Chat cannot be sent while Chelsea is offline. You can send it as a Message and she will read them in her Inbox.

ME: you got offline?
Chat cannot be sent while Chelsea is offline. You can send it as a Message and she will read them in her Inbox.

ME: damn you
Chat cannot be sent while Chelsea is offline. You can send it as a Message and she will read them in her Inbox.

1:03
ME: i will sneak into your house at night
Chat cannot be sent while Chelsea is offline. You can send it as a Message and she will read them in her Inbox.

ME: it will be the last day in your mother's house
Chat cannot be sent while Chelsea is offline. You can send it as a Message and she will read them in her Inbox.

ME: your mother
Chat cannot be sent while Chelsea is offline. You can send it as a Message and she will read them in her Inbox.

ME: hypocritical reformist xtian divorced ass bitch herself
Chat cannot be sent while Chelsea is offline. You can send it as a Message and she will read them in her Inbox.

1:04
ME: what the fuck am I saying
Chat cannot be sent while Chelsea is offline. You can send it as a Message and she will read them in her Inbox.

ME: what is wrong with me?
Chat cannot be sent while Chelsea is offline. You can send it as a Message and she will read them in her Inbox.

———————

I realized my heart was throbbing. I was grinding my teeth.
 "Settle down, Tom," I said.
 I turned off my bedside lamp and threw the cover over my head. I remembered naptime. After I would get out of pre-school, my grandma would pick me up and drive me back to my house. She would babysit me until my parents got home. Sometimes I would pull my blankie over my entire body, in case there was a burglar. If he came into my room he wouldn't be able to see me under my blankie. Unless he noticed the lump breathing on the bed. If that happened, he would stab his knife into my blanket. I would see the knife penetrate the blanket. It would be within an inch of my belly button. He would figure there was no one underneath the blanket. He would leave the room and walk downstairs, past my grandmother asleep on the couch.

———————

That night in bed I was at the lake, or on a lake, sitting in a canoe, trying to push off from the land by sticking my paddle into the steep mud shore.
 The vast blue water was behind me, but I could see it,

and I could also see myself, could rotate every which way as a floating eyeball, could be myself or not. As I finally pushed off I turned towards the rest of the lake but there was now a fence in the distance, apparently to prevent campers from going onto private property. I noticed a person in a canoe, which was actually a kayak, near the fence, and the person was coming towards me, and so was the fence. As the person, kayak, and fence all came closer, I saw it was a wooden fence, apparently founded underneath the water, while the person was a Native American, judging from the complexion of his skin, the headdress he wore, the war paint, the tattoos on his body. I stopped doing anything but staring. He approached me staring too. He waved to me. I stared. He shook his head. He pulled out a bow and shot an arrow towards me, which flew in a perfect arc before immediately falling flat on the water ten feet from me. As he passed I realized he wasn't staring at me but staring at the land behind. He came onto the land seamlessly, hitting the mud, exiting his kayak, lifting it from the sea onto the land. My canoe hit the fence, halting its drift. The Native American took off his headdress, grabbed a bag from his kayak. He put on kind of baggy blue jeans and a white tee. He began walking away past the mud, past the trees, and towards a town that had become visible, with thin two- and three- story houses, street lights, shitty cars.

"Who are you," I shouted.

He looked back at me.

"Where are you going," I shouted.

"To work," he yelled.

He walked away down the street. I turned around and tried using my paddle to push myself away from the wall.

THE JULIA PAGE
•

We were sitting in the living room smoking pot, burning incense, smoking cigarettes, burning more incense, drinking vodka, playing guitar and keyboard and drums, smoking more pot, playing *World Cup Soccer 2008* on Playstation 2, and waiting to go out, as we trembled at the thought of how rare the possibility was that something might happen that had never happened to us before, something that wasn't as abstract as the word "something," and which would deliver us from the monotony that had become getting fucked up and going out, to wherever was out there, where we would get more fucked up, our heads becoming deformed and then euthanized, and that's not to say that was our only course of action, but it was the course we had chosen in light of the other options, such as a family movie night, or World of Warcraft, or a night out bowling with the post-teen Christian fellowship group, or suicide.

I had been out of the mental ward for almost six months. My goal was to return to college down in Athens, finish my three or so years, and move to anywhere. The windows were closed but we shivered, breathing the dead, awkward air. Dan was passing a bowl around the couches. There were three couches in Dan's mom's living room. Dan was sitting on a bongo while the rest of us each had our own couch.

"We should just roll a J," said Tony.

Miguel shrugged. I didn't move.

"That would be chill," said Dan. "I think Steve and Luke might come over," he said, checking his phone.

"I would throw down," said Tony, "But I don't have

enough to make a fat enough J."

He looked around at the rest of us. Miguel and Danny said they were out. One of them said they would call to get some. Tony was a dealer but he didn't have his stash with him. He had been pulled over and busted for possession. Now when he went out he carried only enough for himself. I didn't want to give them any of mine—I was already stoned, plus I wanted to conserve my pot—but I said okay. I got out my bag. I didn't want it to seem like I wasn't their friend. It could have been a D.A.R.E. ad. I began placing buds on the table. Tony put down three buds, so I only pulled out three as well. Danny got out his papers and started breaking up the weed.

"Who are Steve and Luke?" I asked.

"You know Luke," said Danny. "Luke Reklawyks."

"Oh. Yeah."

"Steve is his friend."

"Oh."

I waited without much anticipation for the arrival of Steve and Luke. Six minutes later, the doorbell rang. Luke looked the same, with his American Eagle hoodie and cargo pants, a wavy mat of shit blonde hair on his head. Steve looked about how I might have expected him to look, if I had expected anything. His hair was cut short, but not buzzed short, and he used hair gel to spike it up. He had on a black sweater and blue jeans. The sweater had a small, insignificant pocket on the left breast. I kept staring at it, wanting to jump up and rip it off. Between him and Luke there were three superfluous pockets in front of me now.

I began to create a list of possible ways I could exit the apartment without seeming rude:

1) Pretend to have received a text message, look at my phone, make a confused face, and announce to the group

that I had to leave.

2) Go to the bathroom, and come back and pretend that I didn't feel well, although I realized that one wouldn't strictly speaking even be pretend.

3) Go to the bathroom and jump out the window (it was only a second-story apartment).

I had gotten to my seventh idea (exit the apartment as I fake a coughing fit, in order to avoid telling them what was wrong, or anything, continue coughing as I leave the building, and then sprint for my car once I got outside) when I heard someone say the name Julia Darrow.

"Yeah," said Steve, "I don't really get her. She still wants to date me but she's such a bitch."

"You're talking about Julia Darrow?" I asked.

"Yeah," he said.

I looked around. Dan had gone to elementary school with me but he was peeling an orange and didn't seem to notice anything else. Steve kept on talking, but I wasn't listening.

———

All the oldest kids at our elementary school would go to the Cuyahoga Valley Environmental Education Society (CVEES) every year for one week in the winter. We went on the trip because when my parents were my age, no one cared about the environment, at least around Ohio. The Cuyahoga River was infamous across the country as the river that kept setting itself on fire during the sixties and seventies. CVEES educated us about how the rivers were all connected, and polluted, and how humanity's survival was dependent upon the survival of the rest of the planet. They made their points more subtly than that, talking about canals, taking us on hikes through the white woods to see these canals, which were physically the same as sanitation systems in rural areas, big open-faced tunnel holes in the ground that were formed from mud and rocks. The camp instructors were mostly 30-something New Age freaks. They all wore park ranger uniforms and seemed to love their jobs. One guy had apparently never gotten over ADD or ADHD or whatever they called it back during his childhood. He would spaz out as he led us in this song "All the Rivers Run" at an almost screaming pitch. We laughed at first. I found it hard to concentrate on the lyrics, even when, or maybe especially when, I was being screamed at. My mind was on Julia Darrow. She was cute, but not hot. That was kind of why I liked her. I didn't want Samantha Terry, the really hot new girl. Every guy in the class wanted her, and they all had their almost wet fantasizing hands all over her image. I wanted Julia Darrow—comely but with unconventional characteristics, such as her dark red hair, or her athletic talent, in spite of her evident apathy towards it, or her mysterious family background, living on the outskirts of town, a dead mother and a devoted father, who was the only dad who came to pick up his kid from school, and who was fat, and who talked even less than she did.

 I spent most of the time during that week thinking about those things. We would split into groups to follow one of the instructors on hikes, and when Julia wasn't in my group I would impatiently await the intersections of trails, where I would hope to catch a glimpse of her baby blue jacket (this was in the 90s, before that color became overplayed and cliche). I remember sitting in my top bunk in the camping lodge, slowly humping the mattress. I didn't really know what I was doing—I was only ten—but I had seen it in the movies, at least the small bits I could catch before my parents told me to leave the room. Wet patches would show up on my underwear. I would notice in the morning, but was too tired to care, because I hadn't fallen asleep until two hours before. I wondered if it was sweat or pee. Efficient masturbation methods would come a couple years—and a couple more Julia Darrows—later.

That week was the first time that some of the other kids revealed their like interests. Most of the guys wanted Sam Terry, as I had expected from the start. Initially I was intrigued to hear them vocalize it in a really roundabout way, through games of Truth or Dare and other recess excuses for gossip and disclosure, although eventually I became annoyed for the same reason. It was also almost exclusively guys that announced their likes. Brian, the most talented basketball player and the presumed prince of our grade, had pronounced his like for Sam Terry, the presumed princess of our grade. Unfortunately, his best friend Kyle had the same crush, and he decided to announce it soon after Brian. I offered what I considered to be risky hints at my own likes, but everyone was so lost in their dawning pubescent terror, and I doubt that what I considered a big deal even registered as a muted burp to any of them. We were all more concentrated with surviving that week than we were with the survival of the environment and humanity. They had us play a game every day during free time. It was called scouting. It was like hide and go seek, except that the seeker had to stand in one place, and the hiders could only hide in a certain area. Most of us hid behind trees, and the goal was to sit still and not be seen. I don't know how any of us lost. CVEES was the week that we learned more than ever before about nature: our own nature. None of us went home that week feeling that we had gotten what we wanted. We rode home in relative silence, the buses farting smoke like indefinitely delayed diarrhea.

I was sitting at the church play with Mom and Dad. We sat in the first row of the balcony pew.

All the older kids, including my sister, were in it, either as actresses/actors or as chorus members or both. I figured I would be a chorus member one day, or the star.

They were doing a performance of Joseph and the Amazing Technicolor Dreamcoat, and this girl who was a couple years younger than my sister was the narrator, and she was hot, and I wondered if she liked me, and she didn't even know who I was, most likely. I didn't talk to anyone before the play, even though a few of my friends were there. I just sat with my parents, wondering if the play would suck or not.

The costumes were interesting and seemed like a good interpretation of the musical's fusion of classical and contemporary fashion. The narrator was my favorite part. She had a strong yet modest voice and blond hair. A mood was built, in the stuffy sanctuary. The play was able to make people thousands of years ago, who didn't speak English, seem relatable to me.

I had to poop the whole time, though. I kept looking around to see if anyone was looking at me, but no one was looking at me. The cushion of the pews was old but clean, worn out but the only option available. I didn't really need to poop, I just felt like there was lump in my stomach that could fall at any time, through my intestines, through my anus, through the pew, through the floor of the balcony we were sitting on, on top of the head or the feet of some usher below, who was just trying to be helpful, just trying to be a good person, just trying to make sure this night was special for everyone else, by giving them their programs and pointing them towards the bathroom and showing them to their seats when they got back.

I whispered to Mom: "I don't feel good."

She held up her finger to her mouth. I said it again. She held up her finger again.

It was the part of the play where Joseph accuses his youngest brother Benjamin of stealing a cup from him. The other brothers began singing a song in defense of Benjamin. It sounded like reggae. A bunch of white people were singing in black accents.

I needed to poop. Or I didn't need to poop. I needed to leave. I needed to leave the whole situation. I feared that something would go wrong with the play, or people would start staring at me because I was staring at the narrator, or they would all start staring at me if I pooped.

I nudged my mom again. She asked what was wrong. I said I didn't feel well. She looked over at my dad. I looked over at him. He glanced over at me a couple times but it was clear he was trying to make sure it seemed his attention was on the play.

I said it to my mom again and she said OK and took me out of the sanctuary.

"Are you sure you want to leave?" she said. "You were so excited."

"Yes, I definitely want to leave."

The yards turned green and the sun started to stick around longer. In the weeks after CVEES, I began writing my first journal. At first, it consisted mostly of inane lists, and poems inspired by Will Smith. Eventually, I dedicated a page in my journal to Julia Darrow. I titled it "The Julia Page." It was actually three and a half pages long. I wrote about my previous likes, including one to our fourth grade teacher the year before, as well as a detailed history of my thoughts on Julia. It restated much of what I have already said, but as I saw those thoughts on the page—"The Julia Page"— they ceased their ricocheting around my skull. At that moment, as I looked over the page, they were almost no longer mine. They were just marks with a pen on a page, marks that no one would understand if they were from a different millennium. And after all, once I say or write one of my thoughts, it is no longer mine, because it has left the building (the brain). I kept the journal under my mattress, but I knew it was only a matter of time, in the most literal sense, before I would let someone see it. And I did. I showed it to Nicole Delmedico, who worked the same crossing guard shift as me, and who I considered to be a close, nonsexual friend. I approached her locker, where she was putting on her crossing guard uniform.

"What is this?" she asked.

"It is something I wrote," I said, "I would just like to hear what you think about it."

"Okay…"

She stood there reading it. She didn't make a facial expression the entire time. She seemed to be concentrating. I wanted her to smile or frown or raise her eyebrows or grunt a laugh, I didn't care which, but I couldn't stand the blankness. It was like talking to someone and receiving a voided stare back, as if they didn't even understand what language was being spoken. When she finished she folded the pages and held them at her side.

"This is crazy," she said, and she placed the pages in her hoodie pocket.

"Give it back," I said.

"No."

"What are you doing?"

I grabbed at her back pocket but she shifted away. I kept trying to reach it, and she kept moving away. Our old second grade teacher Mrs. Black came out her classroom.

"What are you people doing?" she asked.

"Nothing," said Nicole, and she began walking away.

I smiled mechanical at Mrs. Black and began walking backwards, before turning around to follow Nicole. She was outside, telling the other two crossing guards about it as they walked to the four-way stop. I ground my teeth. When I said hello to the other two, it was evident that they knew that I knew that they knew something I didn't want them to know. I hoped that Nicole wouldn't do anything more with "The Julia Page", but I also knew that wasn't likely, and I was right. She gave it to Kyle, who shared it with Brian, who shared it with my close friend John. I sat next to the three of them at the lunch table as they talked about me in the third-person. They were making plans to type it up and print out copies, and then sell those copies. I realized I was faced with a choice: either I could tell on them, and lose their friendships, or I could go along with it, and lose my dignity. I decided to go along with it. John was the only one of them with a computer at his house, and so his parent's dining room became the headquarters for the operation. At first, they seemed surprised with my willingness to help them with the project, but I acted like it didn't matter.

"Are you sure you won't get in trouble?" asked John's mom. We were huddled around his family's computer.

"Yeah," said John. He stopped typing and turned to her briefly. "He's sitting right here. He's fine with it, aren't you, Tom?"

"Yeah, I'm fine with it," I said.

They typed up "The Julia Page" and I also gave them my lists and poems to publish, too. It was agreed that we would charge seven dollars per copy, and would split all the profits 4 ways. I didn't take into account the fact that I was both the author and a partner in their venture, and they didn't, either. We sold thirteen copies that Monday before the A.M. school bell even rang. Seven dollars a copy. 91 dollars. I had a feeling that it was selling too fast. I started making restrictions on whom it would be sold to, and, of course, that only helped to increase its popularity.

Word of "The Julia Page" spread across the lunchroom like the plague, and by the time recess came it had terrorized the hill of our playground, infecting even the introverts who sat by the fence under the shade. I should have quarantined myself the moment I put the pen to the page. Julia Darrow knew about it. I saw her reading it by the jungle gym. I only glanced at her a couple times, but I knew she was gazing at me with dizzy anger. I couldn't think. I was dizzy, too. The worst part was I didn't care. I wrote these things, and there wasn't any slander, and if there was, it was against myself. I looked over to the other side of the playground and saw Kyle fighting with Danny, who I wasn't friends with yet at the time. Apparently, Kyle had refused to sell a copy to Danny. Now Danny was ripping off Kyle's shirt. Recess ended, and our gym teacher Mr. Guzman came over, and then he grabbed Danny's shirt. I made my way to the lines that were forming for our return to class. Mr. Guzman escorted Danny and Kyle into the building. Our teacher Mr. Blair came out and opened the doors and we filed inside. I locked eyes with him, although his spectacles were in the way, which only intensifies the act of locking eyes with another person.

"Mr. Maddox," he said, "Can I have a word?"

I shrugged. He pulled a copy of "The Julia Page" out of his back pocket.

"Can you explain this?"

"No. And I didn't do anything wrong." My voice gained volume.

He raised his eyebrows and shook his head. His face got red and he motioned for me to go to the empty art room across the hall. I looked at the art on the walls; it must have been from kindergarteners because they couldn't even color within the lines.

A few minutes later, I was joined by John, Kyle, and Brian. Mr. Blair came in and slammed the door. I wondered what the kids in the other room were thinking. Then I realized that they were all wondering what was going on in this room. Their thoughts were now total speculation on what was happening to me. Mr. Blair wiped sweat from his forehead and rolled up his sleeves and said, "What the hell is this?" None of us said anything.

"You wrote this Mr. Maddox?"

"I did."

"And you let them sell it?"

"I am selling it, too," I said.

"You guys never thought you were doing anything wrong?"

"We didn't do anything wrong," yelled Kyle.

"How much money did you guys make?"

"About 168 dollars," said John.

"Where is it?"

"It's our money," said Kyle, "We earned it."

"Did you know it is illegal to sell materials on school property without permission?"

"That's not true," said Brian.

"Where is it?"

"It's right here, in my pocket," said Kyle. He pointed to a pocket in his cargo shorts.

Mr. Blair walked over and ripped the button off the pocket. He put the money in his shirt pocket. We were sent to the principal's office. The principal must have gotten sick of seeing us in her office, because she left soon after we arrived and Mr. Blair sat in her office. He called us in one by one. I was last.

"I see a guy before me with so much potential," said Mr. Blair, "But you're just wasting it all away. You have no ambition."

"I do," I said. "I don't know. Whatever."

He shook his head. Whatever. I was glad when the day was over. I didn't feel any guilt. I felt embarrassed. We got detention. My parents got called. I got grounded. I didn't care about getting disciplined, but what I did care about was that the topics in "The Julia Page" were discussed so abstractly and so remotely by the people who were telling me it was wrong. It was as if the problem was immediately evident and there was no need to discuss whether it was a problem, and why. Erections were never discussed. Romance was never discussed. It seemed like the problem was more in their own unwillingness to acknowledge what had occurred.

They probably had us stand outside before school so that we could learn to socialize, but we had trouble learning, and they probably weren't being pedagogical, they probably just wanted to get a half hour of quiet before the day started. So we would talk about things. I would make up things like, "My favorite Pokemon card I own is the Japanese Charzard," because it was the most expensive card, or someone had told me that. At John's birthday I said that and he turned to the rest of the group and said, "Don't listen to what he says. He makes up stuff for no reason." And then I would stand there growing angry because he had said I lied. Resentfully, I would commit myself to continuously lying, for the rest of my life, so I could prove that it was OK, because I didn't think he was really pointing me out because I was lying but because he didn't like me. So the lying became a part of me. It was something I practiced before school.

Other social skills we learned in front of the school included fighting, cheating on homework, breaking things, gossiping, and getting bored. We also played, but you don't have to learn how to play, although maybe you don't have to learn any of these things. Maybe they are in us like hate is in us from the time we are screaming from our mother's womb, "Why did you bring me here?"

I know I had hate when I cornered Alex Draper and Billy Lambeau one morning. They were smiling and pushing each other, but their bodies didn't move when they pushed each other, and they had on the same blood red windbreakers with black lining.

I was standing with my friend Jason, and loud enough so that they could hear me, I asked them if they were gay.

"Excuse me?" said Billy.

"I asked you if you were gay," I said.

"What's your problem?" he said.

"I'm just asking if you're gay," I said.

"He wants to know if you're a faggot," said Jason.

"Fuck you," said Billy.

"Fuck you, you fucking faggot," I said.

They looked at me, angry and bored.

"It's OK, if you're gay," I said.

"I was just asking a question."

"What are you going for, Tom?" asked Alex.

"How about: are you gay?" I asked.

"No," he said.

"Well you sure seem like it," said Jason.

"Yeah, you've got a nice jacket, just like your assfuck friend," said Kyle, who hadn't been with us before.

"And he looks like he could suck a cock with that smile," said Brian. I turned around and realized that there were maybe fifteen people watching us.

"Why don't you go suck a cock," Billy said to me.

"I will if you think of a fucking original joke," I said.

Everyone around us was laughing. Both of them had been smiling and now they weren't smiling. They weren't smiling like they would never smile again.

"Fuck you fudge packers," said Jason. "Get the fuck out of here with that sad girly cry."

"Fuck you Jason," said Billy. "You've always been a—"

The bell rang. I picked up my book bag and walked inside. I glanced at Billy and Alex and then I forgot about them, until later that day, after gym class, when Mr. Blair pulled me, Jason, Brian, and Kyle into a room with the other 5th grade teacher, Mrs. Sanders. I didn't know what they wanted. I had been thinking about Julia Darrow on my way back from class.

"Did something happen earlier today?" Mr. Blair asked.

I shrugged, vaguely, and looked around. Everyone else had confused looks, although maybe they actually did know.

"What were you guys doing before school today," asked Mrs. Sanders, the other teacher.

We looked at each other.

"We need to know," said Mr. Bennet.

"We were just hanging outside the doors, like always, talking," said Kyle.

"That's not what we heard," said Mrs. Sanders.

We looked at them.

"Did you say things to Billy and Alex that you shouldn't have?" said Mrs. Sanders.

"We were just fuh—playing around with them," said Brian.

"You can't say things like that to people," Mrs. Sanders said.

"Did you call them gay?" asked Mr. Blair.

We looked at each other. None of us thought we had done anything wrong. We were just calling them names.

"Did you or did you not?

"We were just playing around with them," said Kyle.

"Playing how?" he asked us.

"We were just making fun of them," said Jason.

"Yeah, it wasn't a big deal," I said. "It was the normal stuff we do before school."

"Is that a fact?" said Mr. Blair.

"I don't know what you mean," I said.

He shook his head.

"You guys can't say things like that," he said to all of us. "It's hateful, even if you think it's just a casual joke."

We sat there wondering when we would be allowed to leave.

The next morning when Dad was downstairs making breakfast and Mom was in the shower, I went into her room and took a note she had written that was in the trash. It was on notepaper with designs of trees and leaves and squirrels and a beaver. I ripped off the end with her signature. I took it into my room, chewed a piece of gum, and put the gum on the back of the paper and stuck the paper onto a piece of paper I had. I tried to replicate her handwriting, writing:

"We understand what Tom did and will punish him accordingly." I thought it sounded like her. I put it in an envelope I got from my dad's desk. I wrote Mr. Blair's name on the envelope. At school I put it on Mr. Blair's desk and hoped he would just see it and not really care, although of course he cared. He took me out in the hallway and asked me what it was, the paper he held up, and I looked at the faded green watermelon bubblegum.

"I don't know," I yelled, and he glared at me because he knew and he knew that I knew and glared at him and he knew that I knew that he knew. And so on. Eventually, I knew, I would graduate from elementary school.

The school year concluded without a climax. The Columbine shootings took place a week after we got in trouble for "The Julia Page." I didn't find out until two days after, because I was so distracted with the fallout from "The Julia Page." Everyone wondered what could make anyone do that. Theories were postulated, but everyone wanted to just not think about it, to just make sure it didn't happen in our town. For the next ten years, we would have school shooting drills every month or so. During those drills, we would turn off the classroom lights, sit in the corner, and the principal would speak in code over the loud speakers.

Nicole Delmedico apologized to me for handing over "The Julia Page" to Kyle. She said she had liked him, and had hoped that would make him like her. It hadn't. I called Julia nineteen times one day until her father answered. I asked for Julia. He put her on the phone. I asked her if she wanted to go out. She said okay. We never went out. We never really even talked. I was dating her but nothing happened. The next fall I didn't talk to her at junior high, either. She started wearing nicer clothes. She started putting on make-up. I wasn't as drawn to her after that. One day at lunch someone asked me what had happened with us.

"We broke up," I said.

"Who broke up with who?"

"We just broke up."

"So she broke up with you, right?"

"No."

I looked at her across the lunchroom, but I didn't stare.

I constantly had to find something new to look at, or else my eyes got sore.

ON TOP
·

I didn't really have anything else to do, so I was daydreaming. Usually I slip into my daydreams, and I am not able to discipline myself to get productive results out of those unconscious or barely conscious daydreams. But it is sometimes nice not to be conscious:

I was thinking, This place kills brain cells, at least aesthetically. Too artificial, and not even an appealing type of artifice. Do I want artifice? Do I want to have my own cows and chickens? Do I want to grow my own fruits and vegetables? These things would be nice, but I am too lazy. Perhaps I enjoy artifice. Yes, I will cut this slab of beef-chicken-pork-sodium. No problem. I can cut my own: I work here.

But the artifice isn't the root of the problem. The problem is with the type of artifice. It is too bland. The lights are standard and boring and one doesn't even notice them on the ceiling. The floor tiles, too. What is the design? It is not a specific color of any type. Upon close inspection it looks like a sundry of minerals: little uniformly flattened rocks placed together in the most perfect jigsaw puzzle ever known to mankind. Is it supposed to make us believe we are in a farmer's market at the foot of a mountain, walking amongst pebbles and pedestrian passersby, the only difference being that we have now achieved aesthetic excellence?

No one talks to one another here, except for the workers, and the workers are often reminded not to talk to each other. If a customer is talking to a worker then it must only be for the purpose of obtaining the goods the fresh market provides. It's a deliberate restriction on all social interaction not pertaining to the consumption of the grocery store's goods.

Is this a form of the aesthetic excellence avant-garde artists labored over for centuries?

I suppose it is also just a business model that has proven successful, and most people would say I should stop whining and just do my job. Some might respect my idealism, but they wouldn't really care.

Amy is standing at the other end of the deli, wrapping the salad dishes up for the night. Potato salad first, then coleslaw, then egg salad, then ham salad, then sandwich spread, then the green jello, then the red jello, then the greek salad, then the macaroni salad, then the macaroni and cheese, then the vegetable tortes, then the cabbage rolls, then the stuffed peppers, then the meatloaf, at which point she will be approaching the main part of the case with the loaves of meat and cheese, and she will silently wait for several moments before looking at me to see if I am going to wrap the rest of the case, and I will casually remark that she doesn't need to worry about that section, I will do it, and she will go to the back room and stand underneath the back room's security camera, texting her boyfriend in Buffalo, who she has met only three times, never having sex, even though she takes birth control.

I lose my train of thought as I wrap the loaves. There isn't a coherent idea I am playing around with any longer. I am almost a machine. I pick up a loaf and I carry it over to the plastic wrap. I carry it back and I pick up the next one. I have found that the easiest way to kill time at such a menial job is to keep busy, or at least to keep busy in the anticipation that I will not be busy, and then savor not being busy until I decide to be busy again. It is a cycle of the most mundane breed. After all, time can't go slower or faster. It can't stop. But the mind doesn't like to be alone. It likes to look at objects. It likes to know that it can entertain itself. It likes tasks to perform. Otherwise it gets restless or turns itself off. I have heard some of my coworkers say that they wonder what I am doing when I lean up against the counter and just stare. They haven't asked for an answer, at least not from me.

The loaves are done. They are wrapped. The store will close in twenty minutes. I just have to hope that no more customers come to the deli. I walk over to the cafe section adjacent to the deli. It is part of the deli, but it is also semi-autonomous. It sells fried chicken, french fries, sandwiches, coffee, and pop. There is a sushi section which was originally very popular, but after the first month or two of carrying it the popularity began to wane.

The cafe closes at 8, while the deli closes at 10 when the whole fresh market closes. I work in both sections. There is a cash register that can be used for customers with less than 10 items. I am waiting for Chelsea, one of the girls from customer service, to come over and pick up the register. She usually comes at a quarter to closing. I usually go over there and pretend to be sweeping.

I am staring at her as she stands at the front of the store. She has stepped out of the customer service counter and is supervising the self-checkout registers. Most of the girls that work here hate her. She is the store manager's pet. She is vocal about being a virgin, and how she is waiting till marriage. She doesn't have a great fashion sense, but she has a nice figure. Her face is cute, although her smiles and laughs seem as if they are coerced out of her, which appeals to my cynical leanings. She wears a Jesus cross necklace everyday. She wears somewhat reserved and conservative clothing, and it is as if her sexiness comes with the appearance that she hopes to suppress any sexiness. Her hair is dirty blonde. It symbolizes, for me, her hidden, conflicted impurity. She has long legs, but she always wears pants.

I sometimes feel a boner, or at least some movement, when I stare at her, although I don't believe that is exactly why. While I am sure it meets the prerequisites, I find myself having disturbing fantasies. They are not violent or even extraordinarily perverse: I just want to destroy her illusion of purity. She has made it known that she does not engage in any sexual behavior other than lip-to-lip contact, and probably hand-to-hand contact, I suppose. In some cultures such behavior might not even be considered sexual. But for her it is a whiff of the forbidden fruit. It is Adam and Eve thinking, talking, about the apple. She hasn't eaten it yet and she will not until God commands her. She believes she shouldn't even be thinking about it, but the instant she realizes she shouldn't be thinking about it she has already thought about it. I want to feed her the forbidden fruit. I want to eat out her pussy. I want my dick in her mouth. I want to be inside her. I want to see her clench her teeth, and moan, no more facial expressions that over the years have become mechanical. I want it to hurt. I want to hurt her. I want her to like it.

"Hey Tom."

I look up from the café floor. One of the other customer service girls had come over to get the register. I had become enraptured with herding the food scraps on the floor into four distinct piles.

"Hey," I say.

"Fun night."

"Ha. Yeah."

She walks away with the register. I am glad Chelsea didn't come over to get it. If she had come, I would have felt pressured to say something. We haven't had a conversation one-on-one, or even with other people, because I didn't say much in those cases, either. She is still standing over there by the self-checkout. She smiles at the girl who came to get the register, mostly just a lip smile but a wide one that allows a sliver of her pristine white teeth to be visible. The girl walks past her and back into the customer service counter. As I said earlier, no one likes her. She is the pet.

"Hello, and attention, customers," says the manager's voice over the P.A. "The store will be closing in 10 minutes. Please begin making your final selections and bring them to the front of the store for check-out. As always, thank you for shopping at your Bartlett Street BAM Fresh Market."

In some ways, I find us similar. I am not experienced. I had sex twice and I was drunk. I have gotten some blowjobs, but I lie. I make out like I am more experienced than I am. I want to share my lie with her. I believe she is lying, and she may not even know it. She presents herself as prude and proud, but I bet she sometimes is sitting in bed in the dark, or in the shower looking at the water crash down her body, and she wants to touch herself. She might even touch herself, but she lies to herself, saying she doesn't want to. She is just curious.

"Hello? Are you working over here?"

I turn towards the deli. There is a woman with a packed shopping cart standing in front of the counter.

"Yeah," I say. I begin walking back towards the deli. I look at the analog clock on the wall a couple times. It is almost five till ten.

"How can I help you?"

"I'm sorry. I just need something really quick before you close."

"Oh, that's fine. What can I get for you?"

"Well, what types of turkey do you have?"

"We have all kinds," I say. I walk over to the turkey section and point to the turkeys.

"We have a lot of different types of turkey. What kind were you looking for?"

"Well, I want something with a little kick to it, kind of spicy, you know?"

"We have mesquite grilled. I would say that has a kick, although it's not very spicy."

"It's right there in that bag?"

"Yes."

"Oh, I want mine fresh cut. I see you already have your slicer cleaned. Sorry about that."

"That's okay," I say, even though it's not okay.

"Can you just slice me a small piece to taste, so I can make sure I like it?"

"Sure," I say, with a hint of annoyance.

I unwrap the mesquite-grilled turkey and place it on the clean meat slicer. Watery goo oozes out of it, mixing with the mesquite glaze of the loaf, dripping all over the slicer.

I slice one piece and hand it to her.

She dangles it above her mouth. She bites half of the small slice and moves it around her half-open mouth.

"That's pretty good," she says, "But do you have anything spicier?"

"No, um, not in terms of turkey, no. We do have buffalo chicken breast? That isn't too spicy either, but it has a bit more of a kick to it."

"No, I want turkey. Just give me a pound of that."

"Okay."

I slice it for her. I look up at the analog clock and it says five till ten. I exhale loudly, on purpose.

"Sorry again," she says, "I just really needed this."

Sure, I think, you need this fucking turkey. You really need this fucking turkey. Or else.

"Oh, no problem," I say. I put the turkey on the scale. It weighs 14 ounces. I need it to weigh at least 15. I cut three more slices. It weighs almost 17.

"Please don't go over," she says, after the scale settles at 16 and three-quarter ounces. I throw one slice in the garbage bin next to me. A fly emerges from the depths of the bin. I swat it away. The manager's voice comes over the P.A. again. He missed the five-minutes-to-closing reminder so he changes it to one-minute-to-closing.

"I would have eaten that," she says.

"Excuse me?"

"I said I would have eaten that slice you threw away."

"Oh, sorry. I thought you didn't want me to go over and that slice made it go over."

She rolls her eyes.

I zip the bag closed and print a sticker for it.

"Anything else?" I ask.

"Yes. Can I please have half a pound of Swiss cheese?"

I begin unwrapping a pre-sliced pound of Swiss cheese.

"Oh, no. I want that freshly sliced," she says.

I unwrap a loaf of cheese and place it on the clean cheese slicer. I cut the fucking cheese. I weigh it. It's exactly eight ounces. I'm a prodigy. I print out the sticker.

"Anything else?" I ask.

"No, that's it," she mumbles. "Thanks."

"Have a nice day."

The manager gets on the P.A. again, announcing the store is closing. I jog to the back room. Amy has already gone to the front to clock out. I fill a bucket with soap and water and jog back to the slicers. I wipe them down within two minutes. They are not clean, but I don't care.

I walk to the front of the store. Chelsea is the only cashier left. She is ringing up the same lady's items with that same old forced smile. She glances at me as I walk past her. I raise my eyebrows mechanically. The lady is digging through her purse for coupons. I give a muted laugh which Chelsea sees. She gives me a different kind of smile than she is giving the lady. I want her, and in my mind she wants me too.

There is a squirrel climbing the eyesore but no one notices. No one can see it. Someone saw it, but that was days ago. They felt bad for the squirrel. It was crossing Old 8. They didn't want to hit it with their car.

The squirrel cannot steady its pace. It goes slow as it climbs, but every few hours it starts dashing upwards. It looks down and it can't see green anymore.

"The boat we are waiting for will take us up the river. If you need to use the restroom I suggest going now. You can go in the porter potties, over there by the festival stage. Each weekend there is a festival here by the river, and the First Street shopping mall is abuzz with activity, but there's not really anyone here during the week. The porter potties should be open, regardless.

"Don't be timid, if you need to go: go. I'm just going to keep on talking, but you won't miss anything too important.

"Now, as I was saying, this boat will take us up the river. You can already see the bread factory across the river. It smells nice, right? When I used to live here I'd drive across the bridge, under the highway, over the railroad tracks, right past it every morning. And let me tell you: it smelled delicious. It almost made up for the fact that there was a traffic jam almost every morning.

"Of course, today we won't have to worry about traffic jams. We will only smell the bread for a few minutes, as we make our ascent up the river towards Cleveland. The first landmark we will pass is the Great White Mall. It is one of the largest shopping centers in Northeast Ohio. We will ride alongside Route 8 until the highway verges inland about fifteen miles down the river.

"Now, I am not sure how many of you were old enough to remember the Cuyahoga River setting on fire. It set on fire. Several times. This was the result of years of companies spilling their refuse and other hazardous materials into the river, free of government regulation. You may also not be aware that the fires were a catalyst for the environmental movement and the eventual creation of government branches such as the Environmental Protection Agency. This is true, but it is not as if the residents of the county had been apathetic about the degradation of their waters. Take, for example, that festival stage right over there. It is a sign that residents are again returning to accept the First Street riverfront as a center of commerce and culture, but before its construction about a decade ago this area had rapidly declined from its previous status as a social and business Mecca. Indeed, residents even stopped allowing their children to swim in the river. Citizens wrote letters to the editors of the local newspapers, wondering if their children would be permanently damaged after years of playing in a river that was now found to have liquid with EPA grades barely above a sewer. But this community came together, and now they have the river front festival, which draws thousands of people every weekend.

"Do we have everyone back? It looks like we're still missing a couple few people. Well, I guess I will tell you about the remaining days of your trip.

"Today we will be riding the boat up to Cleveland, to the tip of Lake Erie. You all have rooms reserved for tonight in the Cleveland Marriot. Tomorrow, we will go over to Sandusky to Cedar Point, one of the premier rollercoaster parks in the world. They are constantly in a competition with a park in Japan for the honor of the World's Highest Rollercoaster. Several years ago, Cedar Point finished construction on the Top Thrill Dragster, which at the time was the highest coaster in the world (they had previously held this title until the aforementioned Japanese coaster beat it). The Top Thrill Dragster isn't a ride as much as a tower. It shoots you up into the air 123 meters and then you hang suspended staring out at Lake Erie, before shooting you back down. Unfortunately, as of this year it no longer holds the record anymore, as the Japanese park now has a coaster that reaches 126 meters high.

"Anyways, that will be your day tomorrow. Afterwards, our Dave will bring us back to our hotel down here up the road.

"Is everyone back? Two, four, six, eight, ten, twelve, fourteen, sixteen, eighteen, twenty, twenty-two, twenty-three. Okay, now everyone follow me down the steps to the dock and we will board our boat."

I have always hated Midtown but the bar was okay: pitchers of light beer were cheap and it had somehow managed to hold on to its shitty Irish aura even as skyscrapers dwarfed it. I had been staying at a YMCA in Spanish Harlem while I looked for an apartment. I ended up at the bar when I arrived in Grand Central. It was Midtown, which I've always found completely overwhelming while also oddly void of actual entertainment.

    I felt my phone vibrating. It was Laura, sending me a text, saying she was slightly lost. It was 8:45 and we had planned to meet earlier in the hour, but she and her friend had stayed longer at an exhibit at the MoMA and now they were lost. I texted the address again and gave her more specific directions, although I wished she had just called, because Midtown is extremely easy to navigate, at least geographically (of course, though, the endless crowds of ambiguously affluent professionals, tourists, and beggars have to be included in any trip through Midtown). I assumed she didn't call because we hadn't seen each other in several years, and back when we had fairly frequently seen each other we were not remarkably close friends. I suppose mobile phones have increased the ease of communication, although they have also given greater solace to our respective tendencies towards social alienation. Words are easier to digest when they come as text than as voice, I guess. Laura sent me a text back saying they would be there in five minutes. I asked the bartender if she could keep an eye on my bags and walked outside to smoke a cigarette. The bar had several floors of apartments above it. Down the street there was a skyscraper. As I smudged the barely burning cigarette filter with my toe against the sidewalk, I saw Laura walking on the other side of the street with her friend. I waved at her, not that a wave has much significance in Midtown, but my wave is sturdy and direct, a signal that if it could be written in words would most likely use Helvetica type. They began looking at the numbers on the buildings. They must have realized they were on the wrong side, because they looked over towards my side of the street, a few buildings down. I waved as they began walking further from me, towards the crosswalk. When the light turned red they crossed the street. They headed towards me and recognized my wave. When they had reached my post outside the bar I said Hi. My voice veered upward slightly from its normal baritone. She said Hi, and her voice rose almost to a falsetto, before dipping back down to a normal pitch as the syllable tapered off. We hugged.

"This is my friend Sheena."

"Hey," I said.

"Hello."

"Well, you guys want to get some drinks?" I asked.

"Yeah, that'd be great," said Laura.

Upon walking into the bar I led them to my table. They put their purses down. We stood there for a second. I think they were waiting for me to say something.

"Um," I said, "They have pitchers of Bud for 15 dollars, does that sound okay?"

"Yeah, that's fine with me," said Laura.

I looked at Sheena.

"Oh," she said. "I am going to get a cocktail, I don't really like beer."

"Do you know what kind you want?"

"No, I'll just order myself."

I returned to the table with the pitcher of beer. Once we each had full glasses I raised my glass in a silent toast and Laura did the same. Sheena stopped texting on her phone as our glasses clinked.

"What kind of drink do you think I should get?" she asked us.

"I don't know," I said. "They will probably fuck you over price-wise on mixed drinks."

"You think so?" she said.

"Probably."

"We'll see about that,"

"So, how is everything?" I asked Laura, once Sheena had gotten up to order a drink.

"Good."

"Do you like the city?"

"I do. I am sad that I will have to leave at the end of the summer."

"Are you still taking classes?"

"No, we can only do the program at F.I.T. for two semesters. I have been doing an internship this summer."

"Oh, nice. Where?"

"At this guy's big store. It's a boutique but he also designs a lot of his own material."

"Are you looking forward to going back to Ohio?"

"Yeah, I am."

"That's good. I couldn't be in Ohio anymore myself."

"What are you hoping to do in the city?"

"I am just trying to find a place right now. I started working at the D.O.T. like last week or something."

I took a large sip from my beer. She smiled and took a small sip from hers.

"By the way," I said, "Is it possible for me to crash at your place tonight, after all? I think my friend Shane—you know Shane right?"

She nodded.

"Anyways, I think he is going to bed about now. I should have just crashed at his place but I wanted to meet up with you, too," I said. I thought the word "two" as I said "too."

"No, that's fine," she said. "I mean, we have a couch. It is kind of small, though."

"That will work great. I can sleep anywhere."

Sheena returned to the table. Her drink looked like a smoothie.

"What kind of drink do you have there?" I asked.

"A strawberry daiquiri," she said.

"How much was it?" I asked.

"Um, does that matter?"

"No, I guess not."

"It was seven dollars," she said.

"Shit," I said.

"You like to curse a lot, don't you?" she asked me.

I looked at Laura, who was smiling.

"Sorry," I said.

"No, it's fine. I just had noticed."

"Okay."

"So, it is fine if I crash at your place tonight?" I asked. I looked at Laura but also passed my eyes towards Sheena, to avoid being rude.

"So he is staying with us?" Sheena said to Laura.

"Yeah, if that's okay. I told him the apartment is pretty small."

"And she might fall on you," said Sheena.

"What do you mean?" I asked.

"See this," said Laura. She pointed to a small dried up gash on her forehead.

"Oh, shit," I said. "Woops, sorry I said shit."

"It's okay, you just have a potty-mouth," said Sheena.

"How'd you get that?" I asked Laura.

"I fell from my bed."

"Really?"

"Yeah, it's a loft bed."

"Ah."

"I missed a step on the ladder and smacked my head against the corner of the couch."

"Fuck," I said. I cringed. Laura was wearing a black sleeveless shirt, not a t-shirt, and tight black jeans with brown boots. There was a tattoo on her containing the text of a Scripture.

"What does your tattoo say?"

"It's a scripture," she said. She leaned towards me so that I could have a better view, and I leaned towards her so that I could see it.

It was in Latin.

"Cool," I said. "What does it mean?"

"I think it translates as: And take the helmet of salvation, and the sword of the spirit, which is the word of God."

"Damn," I said. "That's pretty Catholic."

"You know it," she said.

"So are you still into church and stuff?" I asked.

"I go to mass sometimes. I still consider myself Catholic."

"Word," I said.

"You don't?" she asked.

"Well, no. I mean, I go on Christmas Eve with my family."

"I have been going to church every Sunday since we have been in the city," said Sheena.

"Really?"

"Yes. Of course, my dad is a minister, so my brothers and sisters and I were brought up on it kind of."

"Gotcha," I said. "I was raised on it too. I just don't go anymore."

Sheena said, "My boy back home is sending me horny texts."

The street lamps had become illuminated outside the window of the bar.

"I always have wanted to get a tattoo," I said, "but I haven't gotten around to it."

"What's stopping you?" asked Laura.

"I guess mostly my parents don't want me to have one. They always said that if I had money to spend on a tattoo then I shouldn't expect their help. Of course, that doesn't matter, at this point, but I guess I also was taught to fear the permanence of tattoos."

I finished my second glass from the pitcher and poured more into mine and Laura's, which was half-empty. There was less than a glass left in the pitcher, so I topped us both off.

We talked about fashion design for a while. Sheena went up and got another of the same. When I finished the beer in my glass, I made a remark about how we were out of beer. Laura didn't say anything, but she smiled.

"Do you want to get some more?" I asked.

"Sure," she said.

I looked in my wallet. I already knew that I had 15 in cash, but I wanted to make it look like I hadn't realized it.

"The thing is I only have 15 left on me, and I will need to buy a metro card tomorrow. My last paycheck will be deposited in my account sometime tomorrow, though."

"Oh, I guess I can pay for it," said Laura.

"Oh, he's holding back the bills," said Sheena to Laura. "Letting the lady pay. Damn."

I blushed. It sucks not having money.

Laura returned with another pitcher of Bud.

"Thanks," I said.

She handed the pitcher to me, and I filled each of our glasses.

"You getting ready to be naughty, huh," said Sheena.

Laura and I looked at each other and at her and smiled. Up to that point I had considered it only a remote possibility that I might just sleep with Laura, but now I realized I probably could if I wanted.

"Do you guys drink much?" I asked.

"Rarely," she said.

"Yeah, we're pretty busy most of the time," said Laura.

"Although we had a few drinks earlier this evening before we got here."

"What time do you guys have to be up tomorrow?" I asked.

"Seven."

"Nine."

By the time we had finished the pitcher (Sheena had her second daiquiri in front of her), it was almost 10:30.

"Do you guys just walk home or is it easier to take the train?" I asked.

They looked at each other.

"The train, I guess," said Laura.

"Yeah, the train," said Sheena.

"Alright, so should we go to Grand Central?" I asked.

"We don't really know this area too well," said Laura. "We tried to walk here and it took longer than we expected."

"Alright, sounds good," I said.

We put on our coats. Laura's was black leather and Sheena's was brown fur. I put on my peacoat.

As we walked down the stairs in Grand Central, Laura put her arm inside mine. She looked up at me with a smile, albeit a somewhat drunk one. While we sat waiting for the shuttle to Times Square to leave, I put my arm around her.

"What street did you guys say you live on?" I asked.

"33rd," said Laura.

"Oh, by Penn Station."

She nodded.

A man passed us in a hallway in Times Square and he asked if we knew how to get to the Upper West Side. I had stayed up there once or twice. I told him to take the 1, 2, or 3 uptown. He thanked me.

Laura said, "Look at you, doling out directions." She squeezed my arm.

"You guys don't ride the trains much?" I asked.

"No," she said. "Our school and work is in Chelsea, right below where we live."

The streets were crowded as we walked down 12 blocks from Times Square. When we got to their building, I asked if they wanted me to buy some beer, and they responded as if I was joking.

The apartment was a sixth floor walk-up. Sheena said their neighbor's apartment had gotten robbed a few weeks before, and that if I left after them in the morning I should make sure to lock the dead bolt.

It was smaller than I had expected. Sheena had a small room, which I didn't enter but it looked narrow. There was a bathroom. The kitchen and lounge were one room. The couch had two separated parts, and the two parts seemed more like chairs. I imagined them each sitting there most nights, sewing and stitching. Even if the two parts were combined, the couch would have been big enough for only half of my body.

"This should work," I said. I tried to connect the two parts, but there was still a gap.

"Yeah, it's not really for sleeping," said Sheena.

"I could just sleep in your bed," I said to Laura.

"Alright, I'm going to bed," said Sheena. "And to talk to my boy."

"I will just pass out, don't worry," I said to Laura. "I won't keep you awake."

"It's fine," she said.

"Oh, Laura, you going to be naughty?" said Sheena.

"Goodnight, Sheena."

"Alright, good night. Don't make too much noise. I have to get up early."

She went into her bedroom. We heard her talking loudly

on the phone to her boyfriend. From what I could make out, she was telling him that he didn't need to worry for much longer about not having his girl.

"Um, okay," said Laura. "Be careful on the ladder."

"As I have heard."

"I'm going to go the bathroom really quick," she said, "You can go on up."

Her bed had about four feet between it and the ceiling. It was a loft.

When she came out of the bathroom, Sheena came out of her room and whispered something to her. Laura whispered something back. Sheena shut her door and Laura made her way up the ladder.

We started making out and I immediately began putting my hand up her shirt, stroking and squeezing her tits. She took off her shirt. She looked raw but cute. I took off my shirt.

After making out for a few more minutes, I began to kiss her down the chest. I tried to unzip her jeans with the plan of eating her out but she wiggled. She got on top of me and she played around with my beard. I got back on top of her and we dry humped. I put my hand under her panties, which was hard because she wouldn't take her jeans off. I noticed she had a bush. She may have never shaved up to that point. I had never really dealt with all out bushes before. The hair was curly and seemed mangled maybe. I began fingering her. She started breathing more heavily but then she told me to stop.

"Eventually," she said.

We made out and dry humped more. After a while I began to get tired, or bored. I asked her if she wanted to watch a movie before we went to bed. I realized I was extremely drunk and could probably just pass out. She said okay and tried to bring up Netflix on her computer. She kept complaining about how her wireless sucked. We both lay there, breathing.

In the morning her alarm went off at 9. She got up but I was still pretty much asleep. We made plans to meet up later that week, even though I knew I was going to be busy looking for a place and she was going to be busy with a final show she had to get ready for.

I didn't have service in the apartment but when I came out into the Midtown sun a couple hours later I noticed I had a text from Laura, saying it was nice to see me and reminding me to close the door. I tried to remember if I had locked the door to her apartment. I was unsure if I had.

That day I watched people move around on cameras. I saw one man, with a suit and tie, standing behind a post on the subway platform, with his hand down his pants. It didn't look like he was jacking off, but he was scratching, or tugging. I saw an old couple standing, waiting, looking into space at nothing, or maybe at an advertisement. I saw some kids playing around, pushing each other. I saw a lot of people standing alone. I saw a middle-aged couple probably fighting, as the one man kept saying something to the other man, who would respond to him, and the first man would put his hand up and walk away. This process was repeated several times until I turned my attention to a girl in tight pants who was trying to do something to the lock on her bike. I saw a crowd of people waiting for a train that was late. I saw a man in the crowd move away from another man who looked like he might have been homeless.

"Tom?"

I looked up. It was the Administrative Assistant. During my first week, she and I had gotten along, except for the times we didn't get along.

"Hey Sonya," I said. "What's up?"

"Are you keeping a log of the times for things you see that fall under the mandatory archive guidelines?" she asked.

"Yes," I said.

"Because last week you missed two different incidents. One was about people graffiti-ing and the other one was about sexual misconduct."

"Yeah, I know," I said.

"And you need to keep your eyes on it."

"I know," I said.

"It is very important to the Director that you keep an eye on it."

"I know," I said.

"Okay, thank you, Tom."

It was true. I had screwed the fuck up. I had not archived two periods of digital video footage that should have been archived. That is my job. Every day I sit at a desk and I look at anywhere between 20 and 40 cameras that provide security surveillance at several New York subway stations. I saw approximately 250 hours of video footage during my eight-hour shift.

It was a job I got because in college I worked at the college radio station, and then I started smoking weed with the radio station security guard during my late night show, and then he got me a job. Also, during college I worked as an intern for the Ohio Department of Transportation (O.D.O.T.), where I worked on procedural marketing and public procedures, meaning that I spent most of my time moving pieces of paper around. I knew New York needed lots of security people, especially post-9/11.

"Hey, Tom?"

Again.

"Yes, Sonya?"

"Can you please remind Johnny, who comes in after you, about what I said?"

"Yes," I said.

"Oh, Sonya," I said, as she walked away.

"Yes?"

"Could you please tell the supervisor I would like to talk to them?"

"OK. What would you like to talk to them about?"

"What?"

"What do you want to talk to them about?"

"I want to ask them for some leniency. I want them to be more lenient."

"What is lenient?"

"Well, nothing seems to be lenient. I keep getting told by you to keep track of something that I am doing my best to keep track of, and then you come in here and tell me this, and it distracts me, both immediately—for all we know there were ten murders just now that I missed—and generally—I get upset."

"I am sorry you get upset, Tom. Please just don't get upset."

"What? OK."

"OK, Tom."

She walked away. Her job was to take the shit I wanted to the Director. But the Director wasn't there. It was just her.

I looked back at the security footage feedback. There wasn't much going on. There wasn't much going on at all. I looked at Craigslist at rooms and apartments I could live in.

WALLS

•

The floor tiles were that color that is hard to describe: beige but gray but light brown but dark orange but also almost just a plain off white at the same time. I felt as if they had been chosen because of their void mediocrity.

I walked down the hallway without any aim, aside from finding a purpose for the tiles, the doorframes, the ceilings, the walls. I thought I could no longer think a single thought, every thought merging into the next without my permission.

The fourth floor of St. Benedictine's hospital had four hallways that connected to form a rectangle. The northern hallway had a westward erection that caused it to intrude on the uniform four-corner layout, but all that was at that end's end was the emergency exit stairway, and my room.

I was not near my room. I was wandering south along the western corridor. Mrs. Richardson was at her desk on the northern corridor. I couldn't see this, but I knew. She was sitting there with her big scarlet-framed glasses, her fat ass too lazy to move, her eyes just staring at my projection on that security screen. I looked up at the camera and winked. As she shook her head, there was not another wind source on the floor.

I turned the corner.

I stared at a framed print of Van Gogh's Starry Night that was along the southern corridor, thinking that if this was a novel or a film it would seem cliché for there to be that painting right there at that moment. I laughed.

"What are you laughing at?"

I gasped and turned around. There was a short man

standing there. He had on a nurses' uniform. Orderlies didn't really exist anymore. They now shared duties and titles with the women. But as he looked at me I knew that it would be him and not Mrs. Richardson that would have to subdue me if I got violent or even resistant. He thought I would get violent, but violence hadn't crossed my mind. I thought he was pathetic, though. He had a beer belly. He wore narrow rimmed glasses but he looked stupid.

"The painting," I said.

"Oh, yeah," he said, "It's a good one."

"I don't know about if it's good or bad," I said, "But I like it."

He nodded at me. He stared at the painting. He realized I was not a violent threat.

Looking back at me, he asked, "Don't you think it is about time for bed, Tom?"

"What, do I have to go to bed, right now?"

"I would say so."

"I can't just walk around a bit more?" I asked.

"I don't think that's a good idea. Everyone else is already asleep."

"Can I have something to eat?"

"We don't usually go into the pantry at night. Otherwise, everyone would want me to make an exception for them."

"The rules would break from too much bending," I said.

"Exactly," he said.

"So I should just go to sleep?" I said.

"I think that would be best."

"Better than what?"

"Just in general, Tom."

"Oh."

"So what do you say, you want to go to bed?"

"I, um…Can I get some food first? Otherwise, I won't

be able to fall asleep."

"Tom."

"Please?"

He sighed. "Follow me," he said.

I followed him towards the pantry.

Inside the pantry there were baskets filled with fruit, a large refrigerator, over a dozen cabinets, and sitting on one of the wooden counters there were boxes of the small personal prepackaged cereal bowls that you just had to put milk in and enjoy. I didn't choose any of them. I chose a banana. I chose another banana, too. I shrugged my shoulders and looked around the room. He saw me looking at the cereal again.

"No sugar," he said.

"Okay."

"It keeps people up."

"I guess I am done," I said. I walked out of the room and back into the hallway. I stood there waiting for him. He wondered why I didn't walk straight to my room, since it was already clear that I was going to bed now.

"Let's go," he said.

As we neared the nurses' station, located across from my room, I stopped.

"Can I get something to help me sleep?" I asked.

"I don't know," he said. He walked over to Mrs. Richardson, who was sitting behind the long desk in a revolving bar stool chair. I stood where I was, while he asked her in a hushed tone if I could have a sedative. She rolled her eyes. Around the frames of her glasses I could see her skin more clearly.

"Do you know where you are, Tom?" she asked me.

"I think so," I said.

She sighed. I was annoying her.

"Well, we usually have to wait to give out pills until the

doctor sees you, but I can give you something light."

I shrugged. She sighed again.

She walked back into the office behind her. There were shelves and cabinets everywhere, but they were made of plastic, unlike the shelves and cabinets of the pantry. She returned with a Dixie cup. It contained a small scarlet pill. She said the name and I didn't listen to what it was called, and she became more annoyed.

"Thanks," I said.

They encouraged me to go to bed again, so I went to my room and leaned against a pillow. I don't know exactly when it was that I fell asleep.

We were out candyflipping in Kent around the college bars, but none of us were in college that semester.

I wasn't having fun. I couldn't feel the acid. I couldn't feel the X.

I stood near the bar listening to the band play very average music, a mix of metal and new wave and emo and everything in between.

The stage was short and small, and there was a curtain that was sagging at the side of the platform.

Molly was talking to a guy she had introduced me to a few minutes earlier but I didn't remember his name. He leaned over and hugged her, and it looked too playful to me.

I would have felt jealous if not for my exhaustion—with her, with the show, with the drugs, with the city, with the era.

I walked over towards her and the guy. She glanced at me but continued her conversation with the guy.

As I stood next to them, not saying a word, feeling like an outsider next to my own girlfriend, I began to think of ways that I could kill this guy. They laughed again and he punched her playfully in the arm. I kept staring at him, wondering how I could murder him.

"Oh, I'm sorry," said the guy, "If this is your girlfriend."

"I don't care," I said.

The guy didn't listen to my response. He kept talking to her.

I stood there and the guy seemed small and insignificant and she seemed small and insignificant and I felt small and insignificant.

They kept talking. They were discussing the merits of Akron over Kent.

"Akron is for preppy losers and poor people," said the guy.

"Maybe," she said.

"Kent is more artsy and shit."

"I guess so."

"Fuck, DEVO went to Kent."

"But they were from Akron," I said. They looked at me. I wasn't supposed to talk.

"But we're talking about colleges," said the guy.

I stared at him.

"None of us is in college, anyways," said the guy, and he added, "No one that matters graduates from college."

"What the fuck does that mean?" I asked.

"Yeah, what do you mean?" asked Molly.

The guy looked at the stage. "I don't need to get a fucking degree to do what I want to do," he said.

"That's a way of looking at things," said Molly.

I shrugged. It was a way of looking at things, although I wasn't sure what we were looking at. I was silent as they continued.

"I'm in school, anyways," said the guy.

"Oh yeah?" said Molly, "Where?"

"Tri-C."

"That stands for Cuyahoga Community College, right?"

"Yeah."

"I knew someone that went there. You can only go for two years, right?"

"Yeah, it's a junior college," said the guy. "I will hopefully just get a job in the tech industry."

"Doing what?"

"Working with computers. Probably at some business office. Fixing them, programming them, stuff like that."

Molly nodded. The guy didn't seem interested in himself, anymore, after all that depressing talk about community college and fixing computers in an office. I began to understand him. I was the guy.

I walked over to Tony, Nita, and Jack. They were standing near the door.

"We were thinking of leaving," said Tony.

"Okay," I said.

I walked back over to Molly and told her the group plan. I walked away without speaking to the guy.

Nita was saying, "I just want to go home," as I returned. She was pretty demanding of Tony. He made the plans, but she gave the orders. I liked her wavy black hair.

"Yeah," I said, "I think we are going to go." Molly approached our circle as I said this.

We all went outside to smoke and to decide if we should leave, which was already decided.

Jack and Tony walked towards the gas station down the street to pick up Phillies. Molly answered her phone and walked down the sidewalk a bit. Nita and I stood there.

"So did you like the show?" she said. I knew she was being sarcastic.

"Yeah, it was great," I said. She knew I was being sarcastic.

"I'm kidding," she said, even though she knew I had been kidding.

"Me too," I said.

I looked up at the clear night sky and said, "It's nice to have stars every once in a while."

"Yeah," she said, "Do you know any of the constellations?"

"I mean, the big dipper. I don't know where it is, though."

She said something about a star and pointed to it. She leaned up against me as she pointed. I felt the acid kick in. I felt the X kick in. She nudged me with her elbow and it felt like fellatio. The stars neared closer for a second, before retreating back into their proper place. Tony and Jack returned with a cigar.

"We were going to go roll this over at my place," said Tony.

Nita rolled her eyes. Only I saw.

"I might just go home," I said. I called to Molly. She nodded.

"Alright, I'll see you guys later," I said.

"You sure, man?" said Jack.

"Yeah."

"Alright, whatever," said Tony. He was kidding. We had kidded for so long, nothing was a joke anymore.

"Bye, guys," I said.

I walked towards Molly. She waved and we began walking towards the car. I hoped that she would drive.

———————

I remembered waking up in the middle of the night. Mrs. Richardson was standing outside my door. I saw her shadow in the hall outside my door.

"OH, MY LIFE IS SO HORRIBLE," she said.

She was talking about me.

"RANCID BOY," she said. "ACTS LIKE HE'S THE ONLY ONE IN THE WORLD."

I put the sheets over my head. I must have blacked back out.

My waking in the morning was one of those slow-wakings, every half hour or hour for several hours, but I never actually get up and out of bed.

I was up at 9, which was much earlier than usual, but I had also fallen asleep at 11, which was earlier than usual.

The same male nurse was standing outside my door when I finally opened my eyes to the day.

"Hi, Tom."

"Hi," I said. I couldn't remember his name. I wasn't sure if he had ever told me his name. I didn't care.

"You are about to miss breakfast," he said.

"Am I?"

"Yes. Breakfast is served from 9 to 10, every morning."

"Can I shower first?"

"We aren't allowed to let you shower, yet," he said.

"Okay," I said. I didn't really care about a shower. The night before I had been demanding answers. I wasn't anymore. I felt groggy.

He stared at me. He thought I was going to take a while to get out of bed. He still thought I was a trouble patient. He had a talent for disguising his face. His face didn't move, except for his eyebrows, which were permanently raised.

I had taken all my clothing off in my sleep. I got out of bed and put on my gown. I put on my hospital socks. I looked at the floor tiles. I wondered why I had never considered the banality of floor tiles.

"Okay," he said, after I had stood up, "I will show you the dining room, and then that is it for me."

"What do you mean?" I asked.

"It is time for me to go home. My shift is over."

"Oh." I realized that I was making this guy stay after his shift was over. He wasn't a possessor of power. He didn't exist merely to be my male nurse. He was here because it was his job, because it was how he paid his mortgage, paid child support, paid for his mother's nursing home, paid for the Chinese buffet he got every night, paid for the wine he drank by himself afterwards, and paid his phone bill, which allowed him to call the plumber, who fixed his toilet when it broke every year or so.

He walked me down to the southwestern corner of the floor, by the big pantry that he had shown me the previous night. There was an old man in a wheel chair sitting at a table. He had yogurt on his chin.

"How are we doing, Lou?" asked the male nurse.

Lou grunted something inaudible, but it wasn't an angry grunt. It was a resolved grunt. He had resolved to be old. He had resolved to be in a wheelchair.

The male nurse wiped Lou's chin with a napkin. He wheeled him towards the door.

"Help yourself to whatever is left," he said, "I will see you tonight."

"Okay, bye," I said. "Thanks."

I made myself a bowl of cereal, or rather I took a small milk carton and poured it into a prepackaged bowl of Special K.

I ate a few spoonfuls, but then I just stared at the bowl and watched the cereal get soggy.

"Hi, Tom."

There was a new male nurse.

"How are you today?" he asked.

"I'm fine."

"Here is a menu for lunch and dinner." He handed me a piece of paper. "Please mark what you want."

"Okay."

"Breakfast is always served buffet style, but lunch and dinner we get you the food beforehand."

"Okay. Do you have a pen?"

"I can get you one."

"Okay."

"Follow me."

He walked me back towards my room. At the nurses' station he stopped and asked for a pen. Mrs. Richardson was gone. There was a younger, less obese nurse now.

"Hi, Tom," she said.

I didn't like that she knew my name. I hadn't told her my name.

I went to my room. Lunch and dinner were pretty much the same menu. Cheeseburger, hamburger, or veggie burger. Pasta, salad, or soup. Orange juice, apple juice, milk, or water. For lunch, there was also a decaf iced tea option. For dinner, there was also a Salisbury steak option and a garlic bread option. I chose a cheeseburger, pasta, and apple juice for lunch, and a cheeseburger, soup, and apple juice for dinner. I was already hungry. I wished I had eaten the Special K, even if it was soggy.

I gave the menu to the nurse at the nurses' station.

"How did you know my name?" I asked her.

"Oh, Mrs. Richardson told me to expect you."

"Oh."

"I'm Cindy."

"Oh, nice to meet you. Can I eat a snack?"

"Sorry, you will have to wait until lunch. However, Doctor Rodriguez is going to see you soon."

"He's my doctor?"

"Well it's a she. But your doctor, yes."

"Okay. I am going to lie down. Tell me when it's time."

I sat on my bed staring out the window. It sure wasn't a Van Gogh. I could see a parking lot and some woods. The light gray of the highway was visible through some of the trees, but I couldn't make out any cars.

"That's some boring shit," I thought.

Fifty minutes later, the male nurse escorted me to the doctor's office. It wasn't an office as much as a closet, big enough for two benches. That didn't really surprise me. Getting used to the budget of the ward didn't take long.

Doctor Rodriguez entered the office. She had thick glasses. It was the same as every other person I had ever met with thick glasses. People with thick glasses didn't look at me. They didn't even stare. They penetrated.

"Hello," she said.

She kept smiling and she wasn't really paying close attention to me.

She shuffled some papers around on her lap.

She said, "How's it going?"

I asked her when I could leave.

"Do you know why you are here, Tom?"

"Yeah, I came here," I said.

"You're not well, Tom. We think you might need some time, still."

"I'm fine."

"Well, your parents are coming today, so maybe if—"

"Hold on, they know I am here?"

"Of course."

"How?"

"You are still on their healthcare. They are your emergency contact."

"Oh, so why are they coming?"

"To see you."

"I know that's what they are coming to do, but why? I didn't ask them to come."

"Well—"

"I don't want to see them."

"Well, that's your choice."

"Good."

"But we are going to keep you over the weekend," she said.

"You mean, until Monday?"

"Yes."

"But why?"

"You signed a form last night. You're a danger to yourself."

"So? Now it's today. I want to leave."

"I'm afraid that's not possible."

"Fuck it."

"Tom…"

"I, um. I, um. I, um. I, um. I, um."

I was in a fit, indefinitely repeating those two words, and one wasn't even a word. That ended after a minute and a half but Doctor Rodriguez had opened the door, motioning to the male nurse, who entered the room and hugged me with one arm.

"It's okay," he said.

I wondered why Doctor Rodriguez hadn't just hugged me with one arm.

After I calmed, she told me the pills she was going to put me on. I had never heard of them. I didn't know the names of too many pills. They all sounded the same. She smiled as if I were normal and told me she would see me on Monday. She didn't work on the weekends.

I walked past the rec room but it was still locked. I went to my room and lied down. I woke up and went to lunch, where I was given exactly what I ordered. I liked the cheeseburger. It had a kind of soft plastic texture but it was definitely edible.

That afternoon they let everyone except me go outside. It wasn't really outside, it was just a patio with high barbed wire fences on the other side of the dining room.

I lied in my bed and wished I had a cigarette.

———————

Molly and I were lying in bed. We hadn't fucked that night. She had gotten pissed when I drove home. She wanted to just get a cab. She said she would pay. I had to work in the morning and I didn't want to have to come back and get my car.

Now it was morning, and we were lying there, and I didn't really want to think about apologizing to her, and I didn't want to go into work. I was thinking about Nita. I had felt something that night. I had felt some movement.

Molly was an odd choice for me, not in my view, but in the view of my friends. She was a bit on the chubby side, and she was shy and quiet sometimes, but also loud and assertive other times, like when she was drunk. We liked to read similar authors. We liked the same music, but her taste wasn't as good as mine. We liked to get fucked up, but she liked to get really drunk, whereas I liked to do drugs and disassociate. She thought we might have a future.

Nita was different. She was a prize. She didn't seem easy. She had different interests, but some of her interests were more advanced than mine. She was also Tony's girlfriend.

That wasn't something I had to keep in mind. It was already always on my mind.

I turned on the radio on the computer on my way to the bathroom.

I masturbated in the shower, and it wasn't to the girl on the other side of the wall.

When I came out of the bathroom, Molly was sitting up in bed. I told her I had to rush to work. I kissed her goodbye quick and went out the door.

I took my time getting to work. I smoked a cigarette in the car. I parked in the grocery store parking lot and walked across the street into the Doughnut Connection. I usually did drive-thru for my coffee, but I wanted to smoke another cigarette before work. I also didn't want to destroy the environment with the extra engine time in the drive-thru line.

I walked over to customer service and clocked in, then I went to the opposite end of the store to the deli. I went in "the back," as it was called, because it was the part of the deli where the customers couldn't see us. It was also where we cleaned dishes and set out mouse traps. I put on my apron and walked out to the counter.

I was working with Andy.

Andy was in his thirties, maybe almost forty, and he had something wrong with him. He wasn't retarded, but he wasn't very intelligent, at all. He always had grease stains all over his white collared work shirt.

It was no different that day. He said, "Look who's here."

"How's it going, Andy?"

"Yeah. Um, pretty good. Pretty good."

"Cool."

"How are you doing?"

"Alright."

"Guess what," he said.

I didn't answer him. Either he was going to say he bought some new DVD or he was going to tell me gossip about work or maybe he would tell me that he was planning a trip out of town. There was never anything out of the ordinary.

"Guess what," he said again.

"Who are we working with today?" I asked.

"Sophia."

"Nice."

It was a slow day, so I went over to the cheese slicer. I took an open loaf of Colby Jack and placed it on the slicer and switched the dial to automatic. Andy watched me. Slices of cheese started coming out, and I picked them up as fast as I could to put them in a stack.

"You need to shave."

I blinked. I had been cutting the cheese on the cheese slicer, gazing at each piece of cheese as it fell, thinking about Karl Marx's sex life. Could he have had one?

"Did you hear me, Tom? You need to shave from now on before you come into work," said George the manager trainee.

"I did shave today," I said. I hadn't. I didn't know why I said that. I could have just as easily have said, "Okay."

"C'mon," said George the manager trainee.

"This is an afternoon shadow," I said.

"Well, just make sure you shave before work for now on."

"Okay."

George the manager trainee walked away. I shrugged at Andy. Andy did this laugh grunt where you could see all his poop yellow teeth. I exhaled a laugh.

Sophia came in at 3:05, and stood in the back talking on her phone for a few minutes. When she came out I said hello and told them I was going on break.

I went outside and walked around the corner of the store to a bench that was nestled between some overgrown vines. I looked out over the fence at New Route 8. Cars were going by below. I smoked three cigarettes.

I went back inside and bought a small bag of carrots. I ate half the bag in the break room and then my break was over. I clocked in and walked back to the deli. Andy went on break when I returned.

"Hurry up," I said to him, "You don't want to be late for break."

He ground his teeth in some kind of smile.

I rolled my eyebrows.

"He doesn't even do anything on break," I told Sophia. "He just sits in his car with the radio on."

"I know," said Sophia.

"It's the same at the end of his shift," I said, "He rushes out of here ten minutes early, but he goes home and sits on his ass not doing shit. He has no life."

"You don't have to tell me," said Sophia.

"Anyways, how's it going?" I asked.

"I'm good," she said. "I am happy to be here."

She wasn't happy to be there. I wasn't, either.

I let the slow hum of the automatic slicer soothe me as it went back and forth and back and forth.

Sophia had measured the previous stacks into pounds and wrapped them.

Sophia was younger and better looking than a lot of the deli women. She wore a lot of makeup, though—I wondered if she would end up looking like them.

"Are you closing?" she asked.

"No, I am only here till 9. You're alone for an hour."

"I fucking hate this job."

I hummed a quick steady flat note, to show my support. Chelsea from up front came over towards the deli.

"God, I hate this bitch," said Sophia.

I liked Chelsea, privately, but she was hated by many of the female staff, for the holier-than-thou vibes she projected, or at least they thought she projected.

"Hi, Sophia!"

"Hey, Chelsea."

"How are you?"

"I'm okay. What can I do for you?"

"Oh, nothing. I am on break. Just decided to do a round around the store."

"Oh."

I pretended like I was concentrating on the cheese. I had been into Chelsea for a while, and Sophia, but I didn't have anything to say, or at least not anything that I was going to say.

"How are you, Tom?"

"Hey, Chelsea."

She smiled and continued her walk around the store.

"Fucking conceited cunt," said Sophia.

"What do you mean?" I said, laughing.

"She's a slut."

"Hold on, isn't she actually really into abstinence and shit—all that waiting till marriage crap?"

"Yeah, that's the thing. She is into that goodie-two-shoes Jesus shit, but she struts around like a fucking whore."

I didn't really have anything else to say so I just smiled and raised my eyebrows.

"Shit, and here comes Andy, that fucking idiot," she said.

"Yeah."

"Like what the hell am I doing here?" she asked me.

I couldn't tell her.

When Andy got back, we all did our little jobs in order to appear as if we were busy. Management never likes if the workers appear to have free time on their hands.

Sophia's boyfriend walked in the store's sliding automatic front doors. He was coming to get her for break. He had on a backwards hat and a shirt with a popped collar.

"Hey," he said, as he approached the counter.

"Hey, baby," she said.

"You going on break soon?"

"Yeah, I'll go now," she said. She turned to me, and Andy, and said, "I'm going on break now."

As she walked away, I asked Andy what he thought of her boyfriend.

"He seems like he wants to be a tough guy," said Andy.

"Yeah," I said.

"I hate this place," I told Andy.

He nodded. He agreed.

One day Nita and I were both free around lunch, and after getting some burgers and wandering around Target, I drove us to the house of a coke dealer she knew. She said he was married. We got out of the car in his apartment parking lot and we could hear he and his wife arguing from inside their apartment.

"Fuck this," I said.

Nita shook her head and we went to the door and knocked. They stopped shouting and then she shouted at him and he shouted at her and the door opened.

"Oh hey," he said to Nita. He didn't acknowledge me.

"So this is the whore you are giving our stash too?" said the wife.

"No, no fucking way," he said. "Look at that motherfucker. I am selling it to him."

I nodded my head at her.

"Fuck you," she said, and then she started kicking stuff off the coffee table.

"Stop you fucking bitch," said the dealer. "It's not your fucking stash. It's my stash. And you still have enough to put yourself in a coma ten shit fucking times."

She kept knocking shit off tables and screaming.

"Fucking Christ," he shouted, and he went over to her and took her head and slammed it against the wall. I heard the thud. She was bleeding and crying and she grabbed her purse and ran out the apartment.

He looked at us and said calmly, "What's the fucking deal?"

Nita and I stared at each other.

"Well, we just wanted some drugs, but I think we may just go," said Nita.

"OK, go then cunts."

We turned and left the apartment, straight to our car. Nita screamed at the dashboard and I stared at her and then she screamed at me. I turned on the ignition and backed out pretty slowly but I hit a car in a spot behind me. I said "fuck" loudly three times and pulled my car out of the car and out of the lot and drove away.

I liked the cheeseburger I had at dinner the second night as much as the one I ate that day for lunch. It was the highlight of my evening. I still didn't care to talk to any of the other patients, but none of them were really too talkative anyways. The dining room was mostly silent except for a couple conversations that were uncomfortably staggering along.

They had the TV room open after dinner and I sat in there and stared at it. Some people couldn't watch it because it made them too anxious. When these people wandered into the TV room there would always be a nurse in their shadow. I wasn't one of those people.

A baseball game was playing. I sat on the couch.

A lady with black hair entered the room. She sat down in a chair that was facing the side of the TV. She couldn't even see much of the screen but she sat there and stared at the TV, anyways.

"My daughter plays basketball," she said.

"Oh yeah?" I didn't want to talk to her.

"Yeah, she's really good, too."

I grunted.

"Do you play sports?"

"I did."

"Basketball?"

"I did."

"Baseball?"

"I did."

"Football?"

"No."

I had been a long-distance runner in high school—that was my main athletic endeavor. I was average and never was able to push myself hard enough. I remained on the outskirts of varsity during my four years on the team. She wasn't going to mention cross-country or track and field, though. She was only vaguely aware that those sports even existed.

My baseball career had been fairly promising, but it fizzled out after I got beaned in the head. When I woke up, I wasn't as confident at the plate. When I quit, no one was surprised. If I had never lost my confidence, perhaps I would have been telling her how I played baseball, and she would be impressed, or perhaps I wouldn't even be sitting on that couch talking to her, because I would have been a different person.

"My daughter is a jock," the lady was saying. "Hopefully she will be able to get a scholarship to college for sports."

"That's always a good thing to have happen," I said.

The lady nodded three times.

I returned my gaze to the game. She returned her gaze to the side of the TV.

The Pirates were playing the Mets. I didn't know any of the players. Ten years earlier, I would have known the names of almost every player on the field.

I got up and clicked the channel button that had an upwards pointed arrow. I pushed it several times until I got to CNN.

CNN was discussing the war in Iraq. I had forgotten that there was a war on.

The lady left during a commercial break.

I sat drawing striped snakes in a moleskin notepad they had given me that day. They said I should write down my thoughts. I kept drawing snakes that were in lines, one snake eating the next. I didn't know what it meant, but it soothed me.

Mrs. Richardson entered the TV room. She had a guy who was about my age with her.

"Hi, Tom," she said.

"Hi."

"This is Dale. He's going to be your roommate."

"Hi," I said.

"Oh, hey," he said. He had long black hair and he was pale.

He sat down on the couch next to me. Mrs. Richardson stood near the door.

"The TV is fucked," he said.

"What do you mean?" I asked.

He pointed at it. He was referring to the blue-green tint that had infected the corner of the screen.

"Oh," I said.

"The magnetism is all wrong on it," he said. "The magnetism is fucked."

"Huh."

Mrs. Richardson stood smiling at the door. I turned and stared at her.

"Lights out in fifteen minutes," she said.

"Okay."

She left and I returned to staring at the TV. Wolf Blitzer was saying things.

Dale bit his nails and looked at the floor tiles. He had scars on one of his wrists. The other wrist had bandages taped on it.

"What happened to you?" I asked.

"Oh, I was just having fun," he said.

I nodded.

He looked ready to pass out at any second, but when we went to our room a few minutes later he sat up cross-legged in bed.

"Is it okay if I turn off the lights?"

He breathed and said, "Sure."

He sat there for a while and I lied there staring at the ceiling, even though I couldn't see it in the dark.

———————

My worst trip was in the middle of winter. I rode in the back seat of a 1990 Toyota, with Miguel up front and Jack driving. We drove down to Athens, where I had dropped out of college the previous semester, and bought drugs from a friend of mine, before continuing down to the Ohio River.

I ate a quarter ounce of mushrooms. We sat at a table in a riverside park. We each dipped our shrooms in Nutella. We sat there, looking around, wondering when they would kick in.

"I don't feel anything yet," I said.

"Me neither," said Jack.

We smoked a bowl, reasoning that it would calm us down and also might accelerate the onset of the mushrooms. The sky was gray. It was all clouds but you couldn't see them because it was all the same large cloud with the same cloudy color.

There wasn't anyone else in the park that I could see. There was a foot of snow on the ground. The surface of it shined from the sun, which was somewhere beyond the clouds.

"You guys want to walk down to the river?" asked Miguel. "So that we aren't just sitting here at this table in the middle of this field when the boomers kick in?"

"Sure," I said.

We walked down a hill through some woods to a smaller hill at the foot of the river. It looked completely frozen over. I leaned against a tree. I looked at rocks sticking above the surface in the shallow end of the river. They looked like they were vibrating.

"I think there's an earthquake," I said.

"What the fuck are you talking about?" asked Jack.

"Look at those rocks."

"They're just sitting in the river," he said.

"Yeah, there's no earthquakes up here too much anyways," said Miguel.

He smiled and started sliding down the short hill feet first. Jack followed his lead, but he tried to walk, but there was a tree stump under the snow, and he slipped on the snow and fell to the start of the iced-over river. Miguel started walking onto the river.

"Hey, hold up," I said.

I trotted down. Jack walked onto the ice behind Miguel. They started sliding across it like it didn't matter. I crept onto the first few feet of ice. I remembered that when I was a kid and I went to church choir camp during the winter my parents always nagged me about not walking onto the camp's lake, even if it looked firmly frozen There were always stories every winter of kids walking on thin ice and dying.

"Are you guys sure this is safe?" I asked.

"Yeah," said Miguel, "It's thick as hell."

"Yeah man," said Jack.

"You guys want to walk across?" asked Miguel.

Jack was staring at the woods across the river, I made a scared stupid brief little frown with my jaw.

"I don't know," I said. "That doesn't seem safe."

"C'mon Tom," said Jack. "What do you think the Indians did?"

I stared at him. I realized he was always that aggressive but I never really paid too much attention.

"What are you talking about?" I asked.

"People do this all the time," said Miguel.

Jack started walking across the river. I watched his footprints imprinted on the snow above the ice.

"Hold on," I said to Miguel. "Just wait a second."

We started walking across the river. Jack looked like he was almost across the river. Miguel and I were still within fifty meters of the side we had started on. I felt I was holding him back from walking faster, but I didn't really care. I didn't even want to do it. Suddenly, Miguel started darting away towards Jack as fast as he could. I stopped. He passed Jack. He got out his camera and took a picture of Jack. They were almost at the other end of the river. I looked down at the snow on top of the ice. There were Miguel's footprints and Jack's footprints. I couldn't tell which was which. I realized I could die. It didn't matter that I was on the ice. I could die anytime. This made me feel heavy. I didn't want to walk any further. What was the point, if I was going to die? They turned towards me. They could have been yelling to me but I couldn't hear them. I felt my phone vibrating in my pocket. I took it out. It was Jack.

"Hello."

"Tom, what the hell are you doing?" Jack said. His voice was loud on the phone.

"I don't know," I said. "I am just taking my time."

"Are you scared, Tom?"

"Kind of. Yeah."

"Well, it's not going to help, prolonging it."

"I know."

"Like they say in Seinfeld: Like a bandaid: Right off."

The snow was thicker on the ice in some spots, and I continued thinking it was breaking.

"Okay," I said.

I wasn't sure if I said that in my head or to him. I hung up. I started taking more deliberate steps. I steadied myself. At one point I felt like I was halfway, but I couldn't tell. I looked behind, terrified and expecting to see my family or the police standing on the northern side of the river where we had started. There was no one there except the trees. The emptiness of the trees' branches almost caused me more despair than if there had been other witnesses to this madness. It took me around half an hour to reach Jack and Miguel on the West Virginia side of the river. Jack was smoking a cigarette. The cigarette was shaking convulsively in his hand.

"Hey," I said.

"Dude, what was the matter?" said Miguel.

"I don't know," I said.

There was a train coming towards us.

"What the fuck," I said.

"It's the Train," said Miguel.

The train came towards us but it was on the land. Miguel threw a snowball at it. The train made a screeching whistle sound. I didn't know if that was normal or if it was because some dudes were standing on a river throwing snowballs at it. It passed.

The walk back wasn't much better than the walk there, but at least I was able to convince them to pace themselves with me. When we got back to the Ohio side of the river, Jack jumped on the ice just to prove to me that it was solid. The ice crumbled beneath him, but we were in the shallow part and he only got up to his knees wet. We sat back down at the table that we had started at. Miguel opened up his bag.

"Please no pictures," I said.

He pulled out a beer.

"Anybody want one?" he asked.

"Yeah definitely," said Jack.

I stared at him. He tried to open the bottle with his coat. He kept trying.

Miguel pulled out a lighter and handed it to him. Jack opened it. He sipped on the beer. Miguel didn't open one for himself. Jack took his phone out of his pocket.

He opened it and put it up to his ear.

"Hey Mom," he said.

He walked away through the snow. I stared at him.

"How the fuck is he talking to his parents right now?" I asked.

Miguel didn't say anything. We sat there.

"I wish we had some music," I said.

Miguel nodded vaguely. His eyes were bloodshot. He looked fucked up. I was fucked up. A few minutes later Jack walked back to the table.

"How the fuck were you talking to your parents?" I asked him.

"What do you mean?"

"I mean, how the fuck were you talking to your parents while you're tripping?"

He stared at me—glared at me—and said, "Who the fuck else would I be more comfortable talking to?"

When I woke up the next morning, Dale was still sitting cross-legged, with the same sedated stare.

He was the first one to go to breakfast. I saw him on my way to the dining room. He was holding a small carton of milk.

"Did you eat already?" I asked.

"No," he said, "I got this, though." He raised the milk that was in his hand.

"Well, I'll see you later," I said.

He raised his milk again.

After breakfast I took a shower, and they let me change out of the treaded hospital socks and hospital gown into my original outfit that I had entered the ward in.

My parents came to visit me that afternoon. I didn't come out to say hello. I sat in my room. The nurse led them inside.

"Hi, Tom," said Mom. She gave me a hug.
"Hi."
"Tom."
"Hey."

Dad looked around the room. Dale was sitting on his bed. He locked eyes with Dad and then he got up and walked out of the room.

We talked about football and politics and their jobs. We talked about everything other than the fact that we were in a mental ward.

A nurse came in and told us that Doctor Rodriguez would see us all.

"I thought she wasn't here on the weekends," I said.

"She usually isn't," said the nurse, "But she came in today."

We made our way to the office closet.

"Hello!" said Doctor Rodriguez when she walked in. She introduced herself and they all shook hands.

"So how have you been, Tom?" said Doctor Rodriguez.

"Fine."

"I was glad I was able to make it in today, so that I could meet your parents."

"Oh."

"Are you glad to see them?"

"I don't know. I don't care. I guess."

"How are you folks doing?" she asked them.

"Oh, we're trying to remain positive," said Mom.

Dad nodded.

"How about you?" she asked him.

"Oh, this is a mess. I mean, right?"

"Not necessarily," said Doctor Rodriguez.

"Well, we have his grandmother. She is his mother's mother. Out of her mind, and a vegetable basically."

Doctor Rodriguez nodded and looked intently at him

through those glass lenses. I wanted her to challenge him, but she was trained to never pass judgment, except in the form of writing prescriptions and making diagnoses.

"How does that make you feel?" she asked me.

"Whatever. I mean, whatever."

Dad sighed. Mom sat trying to smile but looking like she might cry.

"Can I leave?" I asked.

Doctor Rodriguez looked down at me, such that her eyes overlooked the lenses. I had never seen her eyes before.

"Well, Tom, like I said yesterday, I think you need some more time."

"No."

"Well, I'm sorry you feel that way, but—"

"No, I mean, can I leave this room?"

"Well, sure Tom. But—"

I got up and left. Fuck them, I thought.

They came to my room four minutes later. I said goodbye. I hugged Mom, who was crying, while Dad stood by the door, before coming over the shake my hand and say, "Get better, Tom." They left me a grocery bag of clothes.

I wasn't allowed outside that afternoon. I was glad that Saturday was almost over. It was the weekend, but it didn't feel like the weekend. Every day felt the same.

I went with Mom to see Grandma in the nursing home. I had been out to a party the night before, and it was my day off, but Mom really wanted me to, and I decided it was best to go see Grandma while I still could.

She had been in assisted living, but her money ran out, so she was in the Medicare ward, sharing a room with another lady.

We entered her room and the lady had the bed by the door.

"Hi Judith," said Mom.

"Who are you?" said Judith.

"We're friends of Mary's."

"Who is Mary?"

Mom walked past Judith to the other side of the curtain.

"Hi, Mom," she said.

"Why hello!" said Grandma. "Look who's here."

"Hi, Grandma," I said.

"Hello, Brandon."

"Um…"

Mom cleared her throat. "No, Mom, this is Tom."

"Oh, of course. I knew that."

We all smiled.

We got her in her wheelchair and rolled her down the hall to the visiting lounge. There was a window and outside the window there was a small courtyard.

"Have you been enjoying the food?" asked Mom.

Grandma smiled at her.

"Mom?"

"Yes, dear?"

"Are you enjoying the food?"

"Oh, sure. They cook us something nice every now and then." She winked at me.

"Did you take a bath yet?" asked Mom.

"What do you mean?"

"Oh, nothing."

"My daughter's husband came around earlier," said Grandma.

"I know," said Mom. "I'm your daughter."

"Oh, of course. I know that."

Mom suggested we sing some hymns. I wasn't really into it, but she had brought along the Presbyterian hymnal, so we sang from it. Grandma didn't even have to look at the lyrics. She remembered them all by heart.

After a couple songs, Grandma began to cough.

"Are you okay, Grandma?" I asked.

"Oh, yes. I'm fine. I've always had allergies in this home, ever since I was a little girl."

I looked at Mom. She looked like she could cry.

"Hmm…Look at those flowers outside," said Mom. I knew she was frantically trying to save the conversation. "They sure are beautiful," she said.

"Yes, they are," said Grandma.

I looked out the window at the courtyard where there were five pots filled with some part-dead, part-alive flowers.

I entered the house and some people looked over at me and I didn't know them but I knew the owner of the apartment but I didn't see him.

"Is Tony here?" I asked.

"He's upstairs," someone said.

I walked into the kitchen. I saw Nita making drinks by the sink. She was standing with a guy and a girl I recognized but didn't remember.

"Hey."

"Hey, Tom. You remember Pat and Patti?"

"Hey."

"Good to see you again," said Pat.

Patti smiled.

"Where is everyone?" I asked.

"It's early" said Nita.

"It's eleven," I said.

"Exactly, no parties start until midnight, dumbie."

"Oh."

It felt as if parties were starting later every year. People didn't really go to parties to get drunk anymore. People got drunk and went to parties.

"I have to run to the store and get some limes," said Nita. "Here you drink this." She handed me her drink.

I nodded to Pat and Patti and went upstairs. Tony was sitting in his room with a CD case that had a couple small piles of coke on top of it. Jack was sitting on his couch.

"What are you guys up to?" I asked.

"What do you think," he said.

"Good point."

"You can share some of mine," he said, "But you have to throw down."

"How much?"

"How much do you want?"

"A gram, I guess."

"Um, then 50."

I pulled out two twenties. "I'll owe you ten," I said.

He rolled his eyes, but started cutting lines.

"How long have you been here?" I asked Jack.

"I dunno."

"What do you mean you don't know?"

"I dunno, man."

"What do you have dementia or amnesia or something?"

Tony laughed and said, "I think he's been here for a couple hours."

I nodded.

Tony motioned me over towards the table, where there were six lines.

"Those two are mine," he said, pointing to two lines at one end. They were all the same size. I snorted the two in the middle. I rubbed the leftovers on my gums. There was a little leftover and I put it on the end of a cigarette.

"That shit's gonna smell like crack," said Jack.

"Whatever," I said. He just wanted to do his two lines. He didn't give a shit about my cigarette smelling like crack.

I lied back on the bed and exhaled. I felt light. I didn't know if it smelled like crack.

"We should go downstairs and associate," said Tony, after they had each done their lines.

I finished my cigarette and followed them downstairs.

Pat and Patti were standing in the kitchen still. Molly was here now, with Nita, talking to them. I didn't make eye contact with any of them. I went into the living room.

Tony and Jack were standing talking to some people I didn't know. I got a Corona out of a box on the ground. I sat down on a couch. There was some guy with long mangled hair sitting next to me.

"This isn't yours is it?" I asked, holding up my Corona.

"Nope," he said.

"Sweet." I raised my beer in cheers. He did the same.

We sat there in silence for ten minutes. There was a small group of girls dancing. Jack and Tony were talking to people. I looked at my watch and figured I should get back up and mingle.

Molly was in the kitchen and I felt she didn't really care to see me, mostly because I hadn't cared to see her for a week or so. I had ignored her, and that pissed her off. I went in anyways. Nita looked over in my direction and raised her eyebrow slightly. I smiled.

Pat was talking about the election that was a year and a half away.

"I mean, we just have to get the Republicans out of the White House. Hilary or Obama or Edwards or any of these people might not be the best, but they're better than having another Republican. It's time to get them out."

"I don't know if I agree with that," said Nita. "I think that there isn't much difference either way. Sure, they might be preferable to what we have now, but it would just be buying into the same system."

"So what are you, a Marxist or an anarchist or something?" said Pat. "There's no way that you can avoid the problems, least of all through joining up with one of these freelance independent types of parties. Radicalism never saved anyone."

"But what does radicalism actually mean, though?" said Patti.

I leaned on the counter and stared at them all. I remember being in high school, when I would go to the library and check out The Communist Manifesto and The Society of the Spectacle and other left-wing books. I had had ideals. I had wanted to make radical change. I thought I could maybe work in politics someday. Now, all I really wanted was to go back upstairs and do another line.

Molly wasn't interested in the conversation either, but she also wasn't interested in talking to me. I saw I had pushed her away. She went into the living room and I went out on the patio and smoked two cigarettes, without joining any conversations with the people out there.

There was a stash of leftover burgers in Dale's bedside table drawer. I noticed it one day when I returned from breakfast and saw him taking one from his drawer.

"Where'd you get all those?" I asked.

"They're mine," he said. "They're my emergency stash."

I had never really eaten cold or even lukewarm burgers.

"How do they taste?" I asked.

"Delicious," he said, and he said it with such certainty that I didn't inquire any further.

Music was audible from his headphones. I could barely hear it, but I wondered how he could hear me.

"What are you listening to?"

"Drowning Pool," he said.

"Drowning Pool…they did that 'let the bodies hit the floor' song, right?"

"Let the bodies hit the floor," he whispered.

I smiled and nodded. "What else do you have on there?"

He handed me the disc-man.

It was mostly nu-metal and "modern rock" type shit, but there was the Sublime song "What I Got" near the end of the mix.

"I used to listen to this song a lot," I said.

"Turn it up," he said.

Brad Nowell's vocals came out muffled but audible. We each stared, nodding our heads.

We each began mumbling the lyrics, forgetting most of them, but when it came to the word "riot" we both screamed it out.

We each sang the guitar solo.

The nurses came and stood outside our door. They smiled at us like we were crazy.

Dale and I sat there talking about the landscape. He wanted to be an artist, and he had been drawing the landscape outside the window.

I told him it was like what Van Gogh did, except Van Gogh had a fucking view.

"The view is what you make it," he said. "It is what it is."

I thought that sounded like a contradiction, but I didn't get a chance to say it because there was a man in pajamas standing lurking outside our door.

I turned to him.

"Hello," he said.

"Hey," I said.

"What music were you guys listening to?" he asked.

"Sublime," I said.

"I've never heard of them."

"They're fairly recent," I said.

He nodded. Dale was drawing on his notepad, and didn't seem interested in this man.

"I teach music history," said the guy.

"Oh yeah? Where?"

"At the college."

"Oh, you're a professor?"

"Yes. I am a professor."

I nodded and tried to think of a way to end the conversation.

I heard the pay phone ringing. The professor turned around and walked to the other side of the hall to answer it.

"Hello?"

"No, they're not here," he said.

"Who was it?" I asked.

"It was for Tom," he said.

"I'm Tom, man."

"Oh."

"Yeah."

"Sorry."

I shook my head and went over to the nurses' station. I asked the nurse if I could have a quarter to use the phone. She asked who I was going to be calling, but I didn't know.

"I couldn't find that book anywhere. It wasn't in Barnes and Nobles or Border's."

Jack looked at me and shook his head. "Just buy it online, dude," he said.

"It's not that," I said. "It's just why the hell are there no other bookstores in this town."

"The colleges have bookstores," said Nita.

"True," I said, "But they cater to students. I'm not a student."

They stared at me. They were pissed that I was drawing out the conversation so long.

"It's not a big deal," I said.

Jack put out his cigarette and returned inside.

Nita and I stood there talking.

It was the beginning of April, but it was cold out, and there were no stars in the sky.

"How is work?" I asked Nita. She worked at a boutique.

"Pretty good," she said. "I think I want to go back to school, soon, though."

"I don't really know about that," I said. "I can't really understand what the point is…it seems retarded."

"To get a job."

"Yeah, I guess."

She looked over me. I looked up at the clouds. She looked up at the clouds.

When we went back inside, there weren't many people left. I had a headache. I had shared some of my coke with other people, but I had still done a lot, but that was earlier, and it was starting to wear off.

I could tell Jack and Tony were thinking the same thing.

"Yeah, man," said Jack, when Tony asked if we wanted more coke.

I shrugged.

"Alright, well we are going to go get some," said Tony. "You want to throw down?"

I realized he was saying I had to throw down, because I owed him ten dollars.

"Sure," I said. "I have to go to an ATM, though."

He rolled his eyes.

"Okay, you owe me, though, dude. Don't forget."

"Okay."

He and Jack left. There were four people in the living room. Nita and I sat down on a couple table chairs by the kitchen. They didn't seem to notice us too much.

"What's up?" I asked her.

"Not too much."

She lit a cigarette.

"Do you think there will be anything else eventful tonight?" I asked.

"No," she said.

I kept wondering whose call I had missed, but eventually I stopped wondering. I could see outside my window. The sky was blue and the grass was green.

There were these two ladies, one of whom I have already told you about—the one with the curly black hair. The other lady also had curly black hair, and they were friends, and they wanted their cosmetic products. But the nurses wouldn't let them into the closet, which was a room where they kept all our belongings. They kept arguing about it with the nurses, and the nurses didn't give in, so the ladies did speed walking laps around the ward, loudly complaining about their beauty products, and making anti-Semitic remarks.

The professor got into an argument with the nurses. He kept asking them why he was there.

"Why do I have to take these pills?" he asked. "Why am I here?"

"You're here because you weren't taking your pills," the nurse said.

The professor also was convinced that his roommate was stealing his pants. In reality, the professor's pants were in the closet. He wasn't allowed pants. But he thought his roommate, a skinny little middle-age guy who never talked, was the culprit.

At lunch, the professor was muttering threats across the 20 x 25 foot dining room to the guy. The guy just sat there with his head down. A male nurse stood by the door smiling, looking ready to beat the professor up.

After lunch I wandered the halls. I walked towards the exit door at the southern end of the ward. It had a padlock and there was a sign on it that read "NO ELOPEMENT."

I stared at it, and wondered if it was referencing sex.

A doctor I had never seen before was coming towards me. He stood by me. He looked at me and then he looked at the door.

"What does that sign mean?" I asked him.

"What do you mean?" he asked me.

"Does it have to do with sex?" I asked.

His face contorted.

"Well?" I asked.

"I'm afraid I can't tell you that," he said.

"What do you mean?"

He motioned to the male nurse. The nurse came and

led me away and the doctor exited the ward.

I sat in my room trying to read a book. It was The Interpretation of Dreams by Freud. Dale had leant it to me. I had flipped to a middle chapter where Freud was discussing the id, ego, and superego. I kept staring at the same page for an hour. I wasn't even reading the words.

I heard screams from the room next door. Lou, the old man in the wheelchair, lived in that room. I went out into the hall to see what was going on.

Lou was lying on the ground with wet eyes. A nurse tried to help him back into his wheelchair.

"Get away," he shouted.

He slapped her wrist.

"I can do it myself," he screamed.

The nurse retreated into her nurses' station and picked up a phone and dialed something. Lou was flailing on the ground like a beached shark that hadn't eaten any food in days.

Three male nurses rushed up to Lou and picked him up. They placed him on his wheelchair, strapped his arms down, took him into his room, came out, and locked the door behind them.

Lou's screams were still audible.

Dale went back into our room. I stared at Lou's room, with its shut door.

The nurse who had tried to help the old man up was being consoled by the other nurses.

The professor walked over to me.

"Did you see that?" he asked.

"Yeah," I said, "But how did he end up on the ground?"

"He fell, and the lady tried to help him, and he freaked out."

"Wow."

"Now they've turned the water off," said the professor.

"What do you mean?"

"They turned off the water in our rooms and in the water fountains."

"Really?"

"Yeah."

I walked down the hall to the water fountain and nothing came out.

"What the hell," I said.

"Yeah," said the professor, "Some of us have been talking. Things need to change around here."

"What do you mean?"

"I mean, we are going to take matters into our own hands."

I smiled mechanical at him. His eyes were wide and bugged out.

"Well, I'm gonna get back to my book," I said.

"What's the name of it?" he asked.

"I don't remember," I said.

I went inside and closed the door most of the way. I went and sat on my bed. I could see his shadow at the bottom of the door. It stayed there for a few minutes until he walked away.

Nita and I were the only ones left at the party.

"I wonder where Tony and Jack are," I said.

"Probably at the dealer's place doing lines," said Nita.

"You think so?"

"Yes."

"Well, I should probably head home," I said. I didn't get up.

"Stay a bit," she said.

She leaned her head on my shoulder. I brushed my

hand through her hair.

She looked up at me. I gave her a big wet drunken kiss and she retreated her head a bit and licked and bit her lips. She gave me a soft kiss and we started making out. She retreated her head again and locked eyes with me, and then she gave me a quick kiss.

"We should leave," I said.

She nodded. She was very drunk and high, blood shot eyes and all. I was very drunk and high too.

"I can't drive," I said.

"I'll drive," she said.

I made a surprised face and shrugged. We got in her car.

"Where is your place?" she asked.

"North Hill, off of North Main Street," I said. "You didn't know that?"

She didn't answer me.

When we got to my apartment I opened the door, and right after I closed it I took her and started making out again. I took off her shirt and started licking her neck and breasts.

We ended up on my bed. I fingered her but she wasn't getting wet, so I went down and gave her head.

"Do you have condoms?" she asked.

"No," I said.

"It doesn't matter."

In my mind I shrugged.

"You're on the pill, though, right?" I asked.

"Yeah," she whispered.

She got on top of me and massaged my dick up and down until it got hard. She started moving it towards her vagina. She put it in but I wiggled and it came out. She put it back in and it stayed and we fucked for however long—I don't know exactly—but it went quicker than it usually did when I was drunk.

The screams from down the hall echoed into my room and around my head until I opened my eyes.

"Give me my pants back!" the professor was yelling.

I put on socks and walked into the hallway. The professor was shoving his roommate, the little guy, against a wall repeatedly. He kept screaming about his pants. The little guy didn't say anything.

A swarm of nurses converged on the scene. The professor stopped and turned around, surveying his odds. He tried to make a break for it but they had him surrounded. As several of the male nurses held him, Mrs. Richardson came over with a needle and injected something into the professor's arm. He went limp.

Mrs. Richardson yelled, "Get back to bed," at all of us that had come out of our rooms.

The next morning, the professor wasn't at breakfast. His roommate was there, and he had a band-aid on his forehead.

The water was turned back on after being shut down for almost a full day.

The professor did show up to lunch. Usually, he was talkative, one of the most talkative, talking to people who weren't even talking back. But that day, he sat there in silence, with a dead look in his eyes.

After lunch, I did my daily wandering of the ward's four hallways. I saw that there was a new patient moving in to one of the rooms.

I walked by the room. I could only see the back but I knew it was a girl from the hair and the build. There was something familiar about her physique. I stared at her butt.

She turned around. For a split-second, I thought it was Nita. It wasn't, though. This girl had hair that was highlighted, and the bone structure in her face was more bloated, but it was almost her, it was almost Nita.

I took a few steps back. The girl stared at me. I turned my head and walked away.

I saw her again at group therapy later that afternoon. Her name was Amanda. She sat across from me in the circle. She talked about her problems with anorexia, and how her older brother had raped her at an early age.

"And now he's over in Iraq," she said, "And when he comes home everyone calls him a hero and praises him. No one remembers what he did. We don't talk about it. He's the hero."

She started bawling. One of the women got up and went over and hugged her.

"You're the hero," she told Amanda, "Not him."

Amanda kept on crying.

I thought about how these people had serious problems. They were schizophrenic and anorexic and rape victims. It made me feel bad, like I was intruding.

Afterwards, we did art therapy, which was voluntary. Most days I went back to my room, but that day I decided to stay. Only Dale, Amanda, and a couple others stayed. The activity was karaoke.

I was shy so I sat there and didn't get up. They were playing "Waterfalls" by TLC.

Dale asked for the mic. He started singing the words, but in a deep, raspy death metal type of voice.

"Don't go chasing waterfalls," he yelled loudly but in a low, menacing voice.

I started laughing. I looked over at Amanda and she was laughing too a little.

After I had sex with Nita, I hoped that it would progress into something more.

I didn't call her but I kept messaging her on AIM. Her icon was sometimes green but then it would go idle with its yellow and a message saying, "NitaRXtheHOUSE88 is away from the computer."

It wasn't until the second night after that I finally got a reply. It said she was going to call me and asked what time was good. I had skipped work that day so I said whenever.

I waited with my flip phone on top of the chair by my bed. I stared at it, waiting for it to vibrate. It vibrated.

"Hi, Tom," she said.

"Hey, how are you?"

"I'm good. I think we need to talk."

"Okay."

"I told Tony about what we did."

"What?"

"I had to tell him. I had to."

"Why?"

"Because I love him."

"I love you."

"We don't even really know each other. You're good friends with Tony. That is how I know you."

"I want you."

"Tom, you need to stop. I am about to hang up."

"Why did you fucking tell him?"

"I told you, because—"

"You have to give me a real answer."

"Tom, this is over. I have told you everything."

"I already knew everything. But you told Tony everything."

"Sorry."

"Whatever."

I breathed into the phone.

"Tom?"

I breathed again and then took my head away from the phone and flipped it closed. It snapped and I put it on the chair again.

My brain was fried. I had had hopes with Nita but they were gone. I was gone.

I went into work the next day, thinking it would keep my mind off of Nita. It didn't. It was a Sunday and it was very busy. There was a crowd of over 30 people on the other side of the counter, waiting for me to cut their meat. I kept thinking I would see someone I knew, someone who also knew Tony and/or Nita and or just someone who had heard about me fucking my best friend's girlfriend.

I went on break once the crowd died down. I got in my car and drove away. I didn't go back.

———————

Doctor Rodriguez was sitting across from me with those eyes and those eyeglasses.

"I have some news, Tom," she said.

I raised my eyebrows and tilted forward. "What?" I thought. "Get on with it."

She was looking at a clipboard.

"We are going to let you leave tomorrow," she said.

"Really?" I asked.

"Yes. There is only one condition."

"What?"

"That you go home with your parents."

I had rejected this plan earlier in the week. Now it had

been a week and I realized it was my only choice.

"Okay," I said. "That's fine."

I told Dale afterwards and he said, "Congratulations" in one of the least congratulatory voices I had ever heard.

He informed me that he was leaving that day, too, except he wasn't leaving the hospital. He was just going to a different ward.

"They'll have better food," he said.

"We should stay in touch," I said.

"Yeah, man," he said.

He wrote down the URL for his Myspace. I took it and said I would add him. I forgot that I didn't use Myspace anymore. I had deleted my account the week before.

———————

I deleted all my social media accounts, and lied on the couch of my apartment. I didn't want to know anyone that I knew, not if they would have to know me as the person I was.

I went to the liquor store and bought a case of vodka. I went to my dealer's apartment and bought some coke, valium, oxycodone, mushrooms, and acid. I was about to leave when I realized I had forgotten to buy pot.

I had spent half the money in my bank account, and it wasn't like there was going to be a cash injection, because I planned to take as long as I wanted off of work.

I was drunk and high every day for 6 days straight. On the seventh day, I woke up and drank a cup of tea. As I smoked my first cigarette of the day, I looked outside. There wasn't a yard outside my window. There were just a bunch of overgrown weeds and some trash.

I decided to go to my parents' house. I couldn't find my car keys, so I decided to just take the bus. I rode along Old

Route 8 north towards the Falls. We went over the High Level Bridge. I got off the bus at Broad Street. I walked down the hill a few blocks to the house I had grown up in. The key was in its normal place, inside the garage's exterior lamp.

I turned on the TV and skimmed through the channels. There was nothing. I went upstairs and opened the medicine cabinet. I saw there was some vicodin left from when Dad had had surgery to remove cancer the year before.

I took the bottle of pills downstairs. There was some orange juice on top of the freezer. I got out my flask and made a screwdriver. I swallowed the 17 pills that were in the bottle.

I remember sitting back down in front of the TV, trying to find a channel and then I blacked out, and the next thing I remembered was waking up in the emergency room after getting my stomach pumped.

———————

Amanda came over and kissed me on the cheeks as I was leaving the ward with my parents. I hadn't really talked to her, but she seemed in a lighter mood than she had been the previous days.

The two crazy ladies with black hair were still complaining about their cosmetic products.

Lou was sitting in his wheelchair again, and there wasn't any animation to his eyes anymore.

"I never said thank you," I said to Mom, as we walked into the parking lot.

"For what?" she asked.

"For finding me that day. For calling 911."

"Oh, you know there is no need to thank me."

"I'm sorry," I said.

"You don't need to apologize," she said.

"We are just glad you are better," said Dad.

I looked out the window of the car at the wooden fence along the road.

"I, um," I said. "I don't know what I was going to say."

As I walked into the house with Mom and Dad, I felt relieved, renewed, knowingly and happily a walking cliché, eager for my second chance at life.

It was not long before that ended. I felt pathetically contained in my old room at my parents' house, while my sister was off in a different state living what one could consider the normalcy of adult life. It was as if I had to go back in life, almost like learning to walk again.

I walked outside one day late that spring and lit a cigarette and walked down the boulevard to the local elementary school that I had attended. A class was out for recess. Several girls and a boy sat atop a jungle gym talking. The rest of the class was on the pavement courts preparing a kick ball game. I remembered that my friends and I had once stood on those same courts and said someday we would start the first professional kick ball league, which of course we didn't. I watched as the two captains gleefully choose who would be on their team. Each child would smile with pride or frown with disgust depending on whether they liked the team that had chosen them.

DIFFERENT SIZE BEDS

•

We drove down into the boonies. The eastern edge of Ohio is historically Pennsylvania Dutch. There are lots of Amish people living around there. The Amish are the extreme. They don't use electricity. Mom's family was from around there. They were pretty religious but they weren't Amish. We passed a horse and carriage.

I never wondered how Dad was able to get around that area. We could go for miles and miles without seeing any signs, and when we did it was all the same three or four German surnames. There were constantly back roads, mostly dirt ones, but none of them had markings and I didn't know where they led.

The restaurant we always went to was called The Rhine Kitchen. There were all these Amish people back in the kitchen cooking food without electricity. The dining room was the size of half a football field. None of the customers were Amish. We were all people from the cities and suburbs there on a one-day vacation.

We sat at a table. It was me, Mom, Dad, and Rachel. I was eating a hot dog with mustard when I heard one waitress saying something to another waitress in a language I didn't understand.

"Why don't they just speak English?" I said.

"Stop it," said Mom.

"That's rude," said Dad.

I had rhubarb pie for dessert. Mom, Dad, and Rachel shared a bowl of hot pecan pudding. I felt like a spoiled brat for eating my own dessert. Mom and Dad said it was okay, but Rachel gave me a look as if to say it wasn't okay.

We went to a gift shop. They sold Christian-themed music, different kinds of furniture, a zillion different quilts, Christmas decorations, and other random knick-knacks.

I followed Dad around as he browsed with no particular purpose, except when he found the New Age CD section, but even then he didn't plan on buying anything. Mom and Rachel were elsewhere shopping with greater interest.

The Jehovah's Witnesses were knocking on doors across the street. I ran to the front door and made sure it was locked. I ran up to the second floor to my sister's room. I watched them knock on Marty's house. No one answered the door. They walked over to the next house. Marty peeked out one of his windows. They knocked on the next house. Dorothy, the old lady who lived there, answered the door. She said something to them. They started talking. It went on for a few minutes. I wondered what they were talking about. I was nine, and I had usually had a baby sitter before. I wondered if I still needed baby sitters. The Witnesses handed Dorothy some pamphlets. She went back inside.

They started walking towards me. There were some squirrels running around in circles after one another in the yard. They scattered when the Witnesses came up the driveway. I repositioned myself below the window. I didn't want them to see me if they looked up. They rang the doorbell. It vibrated in my ear. They rang it twice more. It vibrated in my ear, twice more. I heard them talking to each other. Their voices got louder.

"We're not interested," I heard one of them say.

I looked out the window. Mom, Dad, and Rachel were outside.

"No," said Dad. "We're not interested."

The Witnesses walked away. They walked along the sidewalk towards the next house. If they had walked through the lawn, I am sure that Dad would have yelled at them. He yelled at the paperboy and substitute mailmen when they would walk through the lawn. The regular mailman knew not to walk in the lawn. I wondered if the Witnesses didn't walk through the lawn because they had good manners or if they just didn't want to stain their shoes.

"We're home," said Mom.

I walked downstairs. Rachel was sobbing.

"Hi," I said.

"Hi, Tom," she said.

"What's up?"

"Not a whole lot. We are talking to your sister. Can you please go up to your room?"

I went up to my room. I made sure my steps were loud so that it was obvious I went to my room. I tip toed back towards the stair well. I heard Rachel talking as she sobbed.

"But he said that I could come audition again, but in LA the next time," she said, "And there would be a good chance I could join his line."

"Rachel," Mom said, "I know you really want this, but it's not at all certain."

"It's a long shot," said Dad.

"But why can't you guys just believe I'll be able to do it?"

"Because it's all very vague, honey. There's no way of knowing you wouldn't end up wasting a lot of time and money."

"You know, Rachel," said Dad, "Sometimes we just have to give up on some of our dreams."

"Lindsey's parents believe in her," said Rachel.

"Well, that's Lindsey's parents, not us," said Mom.

"I know," said Rachel. "That's obvious."

I didn't remember ever hearing Rachel cry like that. She must have cried a lot when she was younger, but the memories were vague. She had just finished junior high, and I couldn't distinctly remember her ever crying.

"Rachel," said Dad, "We do believe in you."

"Yeah," said Mom.

"But we just don't think this a good idea," said Dad. "You need to understand that you're a smart girl. There are so many other things you can do."

"But why can't you let me do this?"

"Because we love you," said Mom. "And we don't want to let you throw away other opportunities."

"We're trying to protect you," said Dad. "You don't know how many girls this guy said that to—he may have said it to hundreds just in the past week."

Rachel continued sobbing.

I tip toed back to my room. Later Mom came up and asked how my day had been. I asked if I could go downstairs, because I wanted to go play basketball. She said okay.

I dribbled the ball as I walked up the hill to the elementary school park. I got to the court and began playing with some guys I knew from the neighborhood. They had already been playing all afternoon and they quit after a few minutes and went home.

I took the ball in my hand and walked to half court. I ran towards the basket with the ball in my hand. When I got within a few yards of the hoop I tried to dunk the ball. I couldn't dunk it. I threw it desperately at the hoop. It slammed against the bottom of the rim and hit my legs from behind. I fell to the ground. When I got up there were scratches on my legs. They were going to become scabs. I liked scabs, though.

That night I was watching an NBA game with dad. They listed the starting lineup for each team. The shortest player was 6 foot four. I was 4 foot ten at the time. I remembered that Mugsy Bogues was 5 foot three, but I knew he was an exception.

"The Treaty of Greenville in 1795 created the new western frontier for the United States. The treaty line began at the mouth of the Cuyahoga River in present-day Cleveland. It ran south along the river to the portage between the Cuyahoga River and Tuscarawas River, in what is now known as the Portage Lakes area between Akron and Canton."

"Thank you, Jessie," said Mr. Csonka.

We all looked up from our textbooks, which were about the history of Ohio, which was the statewide fourth grade social studies curriculum.

"Now," said Mr. Csonka, "You all know that the portage they are referring to here is now Portage Trail, right? It's just down the road there."

"By the Cathedral of the Resurrected Angels?" asked a kid.

"Yep, right down that street," said Mr. Csonka, pointing outside at Old 8. "At the corner of Old 8 and Portage Trail. It's where Marvin Eisley preaches."

"Who's he?" asked a girl.

"He's that guy with the funny commercials," said the boy.

"Yeah," said Mr. Csonka, "He's the guy who always goes: LET THE SPIRITS COME OUT! He brings in sick people and stands over them and waves his hands and says that. A lot."

I laughed. Most of the class laughed.

"Who goes to his church?" asked the girl.

"Oh, crazy people," said Mr. Csonka.

We laughed.

"How did you say he does that?" someone asked.

"LET THE SPIRITS COME OUT!"

Mr. Csonka got on the table and repeated, "LET THE SPIRITS COME OUT! I SAID COME OUT YOU DEMONS!"

We laughed.

"He's a character, alright," said Mr. Csonka.

"His commercials are funny," said another kid.

"Let's get back to the reading," said Mr. Csonka. "I want you to flip ahead to page 140. We will now be moving ahead to the War of 1812."

We read about the War of 1812. We read about Tecumseh creating a Confederation of Indians in order to finally stop the westward expansion of the United States. Mr. Csonka asked if we had any questions.

"When do we get to go on our field trip up the Cuyahoga to Cleveland?" I asked.

"That doesn't really matter right now, does it?" he said.

"I don't know," I said.

"What's that on your shirt?" he asked, pointing.

I looked down.

"PSYCH!" he said.

The class laughed. I blushed. He did that joke a lot. I had no idea how anyone fell for it anymore. It had gotten popular and we all liked to do it to each other at recess, too.

After class we went to recess. We always played kick ball. Mr. Csonka was standing by the court talking to another teacher. He had chosen two of the people that were good but weren't allowed to be captains, probably because they were talented but not divisive. They picked teams. Timothy Thorpe was the last one not to be picked. He was one of the kids who had to go to a tutor for help with writing. Each captain said, "You can have him," to the other captain.

"Hold on," I said. "Why don't we just make it luck to decide who gets him?"

"What do you mean?" asked my captain.

"I mean, we ask him a question, if he gets it right he's on our team, if not, he's yours."

"What question?" asked the other captain.

"It will be easy," I said.

"Go ahead, then."

"Tim, can you tell me what year, or years, the War of 1812 was fought in?"

He looked at me. He scrunched his face.

"Um, I don't care," he said.

"C'mon, Timothy," I said. "Just answer it. The War of 1812: when was it?

"1812," he said.

"Wrong! It was actually from 1812 to 1815. You only got one year right."

He blushed. I felt shitty and good.

"Okay Timothy," said the other captain, "You can be on our team."

The game of kickball was fun. I had gotten better. I had gotten made fun of when I was younger but now I was developing into a solid player. My team was winning by 2 points with only ten minutes left in recess. Mr. Csonka decided to guest-kick for the other team. He came to home base, almost twice as tall as any of us. My team protested but he told us it was just a game. He kicked it over one of the fences and it took us a couple minutes to retrieve it. Meanwhile, Mr. Csonka and the two people who were on base made it to home. We didn't get another chance to go on offense again. The other team won.

The next day, Sock and I were caught filling one of the toilets with rolls of toilet paper. I don't know why. We were going to flush the rolls down the toilet but before we could Mr. Csonka caught us.

"C'mon guys," he said. "What are you doing?"

"I don't know," we each said.

"I'm gonna have to give you a detention tonight. And you should apologize to the janitor for making his job harder."

After we got out of the detention that afternoon, I walked with Sock through the school parking lot. A car was coming up behind us. I hurried out of the way into the grass. Sock kept walking in a straight line through the parking lot into the grass.

"You should move," I said. "That car could hit you."

"Let them," he said, "I'll sue their asses."

———

"Wasn't Jefferson actually conservative? He wanted a smaller government. He opposed the National Bank. He didn't want a big federal government. It seems closer to the Republicans of today."

"I disagree. First of all, it was a different time. But Jefferson supported democratic rights. He was opposed to the Alien and Sedition Acts, a series of laws that bore an eerie resemblance to the Patriot Act that was just passed."

"I don't understand. Both parties passed that, I think almost unanimously."

"I don't know about that. But what I am basically trying to tell you is that he had a spirit of democracy about him that has carried forward to the Democratic Party of today."

"That doesn't make any sense."

"I don't know how I can help you to see, Mr. Maddox...."

"I mean, I guess I just don't see how Jefferson's legacy can be seen in the Democrats of today."

"Well, if you look at President Bush with his immediate resolve to go to war. Jefferson was deeply opposed to America's undeclared naval war with France in the 1790s. It's so similar to today."

"I hate those towel-heads."

"Excuse me Ms. Ispen?"

Mumbles.

"Okay, we need to move on but do you see what I am talking about Mr. Maddox?"

"No, not really. Jefferson expanded the country with the Louisiana Purchase, which of course meant they had to fight with the Indians, and Madison, his protégé, went to war with England. Those were acts of military aggression. I don't know."

"I'm sorry. But we do need to move on. The Election of 1801. Running for the Federalists was President Adams. His main competitor was Jefferson, running for what we will call the (Democratic)-Republican party. Now back the electoral college—Yes, Mr. Maddox…"

"I just think it would make more sense to just call it the Republican Party. That is what it was called. I understand that that party went defunct and then a new Republican Party was formed, but it just feels like you're making up history somewhat."

"Well, Mr. Maddox, perhaps you would like to come teach the class?"

"What?"

"I mean, come up here and lecture."

"About anything?"

"No about these notes on the overhead that we need to get through, but you keep interrupting. So perhaps if you just led the lecture everything would go a lot smoother."

"Um."

"That doesn't sound like fun?"

"No."

"Why not?"

"Fine."

"What?"

"I'll do it."

I got up and walked to the front of the room. He gave a smug smile and glared at me through those glasses as I approached the front. He handed me the marker he had been using. The lights were off so that the overhead projector's glare could be undeniably clear against the white screen pulled down in front of the blackboard. It was difficult to see my friends. I saw Kyle smiling near the front of his row, in the middle of the alphabet. I couldn't see Brian, in the back of that row, also near the middle of the alphabet.

"Um, yeah. First we have…"

I looked out into the classroom. Kyle was laughing. Some of the students were wide-eyed, while others were falling asleep. I stood there saying "um" repeatedly like a malfunctioning robot trying to say "umbrella."

"I give up," I said. I handed the marker back to him and sat down.

"Now you know what I have to deal with, Mr. Maddox. Please keep that in mind. Where were we? Oh, right— the election of 1800."

Mr. Pinto was my science teacher and he was a liberal, I thought, and I fucking hated liberals. I hated liberals and Democrats. I was a Republican and a conservative. I also wouldn't be able to vote for another 5 years.

"What are you?" I asked him one day, when he mentioned something about the environment.

"What do you mean?"

"I mean are you a Democrat?"

"I don't support any political parties. Or at least I'm not a member of any political party."

"But are you liberal or conservative?"

"I don't think I'm either."

"What do you mean?"

"I don't identify with any political ideology."

It didn't make sense to me. I broke the end of my pencil against my desk.

Later that week, I found out I was chosen to go to a Leadership Conference, which was confusing, because I didn't think anyone looked up to me as a leader, and I probably thought that because no one did. I didn't really even have friends. I hated middle school. I hated getting boners and having to move to adjust them to go upwards towards my belt, so the belt could hold down the tip of the boner and make sure it didn't stick out. I hated that I had to pick at pimples—new ones every day—but also not pick at pimples, because that would just make them bleed, and then leave scars, and no one wanted to look at that. I hated that I didn't want to talk to my parents but didn't want to be mean about it but couldn't figure out another way to go about it, because they were just so nice and kind. I hated that Al Gore had almost stolen the election from Bush. I hated that the music I liked a lot really sucked, and I knew it, it was just a matter of time until I gave up on it. I would sit or stand around my parent's house, singing Limp Bizkit songs or Blink-182 songs. At the time, it was not apparent that, in many ways, both groups were reactionary, or at least associated with trends that were reactionary, the result of ennui from Reagan and Clinton, and symptomatic of the Bush years. Years later, I would look back on my earlier self and my earlier music taste, and I would hate it all.

But right then I just hated right then. I was at the leadership conference, and we split into groups to talk about leadership in light of 9/11. A speaker talked about precautions we could take for the holidays that were approaching, and what we could say if we thought we saw something odd at the airport or the mall. We split into small groups with two teachers leading each group. Mr. Pinto and Mrs. Perkins were the chaperones from my school, and Mrs. Perkins was one of the teachers leading the group I was in. The other was a lady from one of the inner-city schools named Ms. Graham. They asked us what we thought about the reasons for the attack. They asked us what we thought America should do to solve the problem.

Ms. Graham was saying, "I think maybe we need to understand the psychology of the terrorists."

Mrs. Perkins said, "What do you guys think? What actions should we take?"

A kid from a farm town said, "I don't get why all those people were cheering when the attacks happened."

"Well, that's a good question," said Ms. Graham. "What do you guys think?"

"I think they are mean and rude people," said a girl named Krista from one of the other schools in my area.

"What makes you think that?"

"How could they celebrate such a horrible thing? It's just horrible."

"Anyone else?" asked Ms. Graham.

"I don't think we can really sit around trying to think about why they did it," I said.

"What do you think we should do instead?" asked Ms. Graham.

"I think we need to go and take over all these countries. All these different countries. Any country with Muslims or dictators—we need to go and occupy them and make them democracies."

Ms. Graham looked at me scared and slowly said, "I'm not sure if we could do that."

"Well then, we need to try," I said.

"Have you considered the other side?" asked Mrs. Perkins.

"No, not really," I said.

"Well, you may want to at some point. That's what makes us leaders."

"Can I say one thing," said Krista.

"Yes," said Mrs. Perkins.

"I don't understand why they are trying to make us afraid."

"Who? The terrorists?"

"No, the government. We need to move on. We can't live our lives in fear."

"Can you give an example?"

"This conversation right here. About how to prepare for and prevent future attacks. It's making us all afraid. It's what the government wants."

"Do you guys think so?"

A few people nodded their heads. I didn't know and I didn't say anything.

"Well, there's not much else to do, you know? There ain't a whole lot else I can do. I've got screws loose, literally. They screwed it up and then it came unscrewed again. They said they wouldn't screw it back up again but who cares, right? Because they already screwed me. That's why I walk around a lot, I guess. Trying to see as many things and people, trying to remember what it felt like."

I was sitting with Sock and Sean on the steps in front of our church.

"Have you been here all afternoon, Bruce?" asked Sean.

"I'm still finishing my coffee," he said.

He held up his coffee cup. It was the same cups they used in the parlor below the sanctuary. People would go down there after the services and drink coffee and eat doughnuts. The service ended nine hours before. His coffee was cold.

"Did you go to either of the services today, Bruce?" I asked.

"No, I just sat down in the basement."

"Oh, why's that?" asked Sean.

"I don't know," said Bruce. He started scratching his head, rapidly. His nails were twice as long as any I had ever seen—even women didn't have them that long.

"Ok," said Sean.

"I mean, I like the church. But I feel bad walking into the sanctuary with my dirty clothes and shit. Plus, I cough and talk to myself sometimes. I can't help it, but I don't like sitting there, even at the back, where I usually sit."

We had twenty minutes until choir practice.

"I like going down there, and talking to people," said Bruce. "Drinking my coffee and mingling with all the different people."

I raised my eyebrows. I couldn't remember having ever seen anyone go up and talk to him. We would usually go down there and steal doughnuts without paying the fifty cents that the sign recommended, so we usually jetted out pretty soon. But usually I saw Bruce kind of wandering around. No one would talk to him and if he went up to talk to people they tried to talk to him but left soon after.

"We should probably head in for choir," said Sean.

"Yeah," I said. Sock nodded.

"See you later, Bruce," I said.

"Oh, you fellows heading in?"

"Yep," said Sean.

"Alright, have a nice day."

"You okay to get home, Bruce?" I asked.

"Yeah, I'll be fine. I just got a long walk."

"Where do you live?" asked Sean.

"In those apartments down on Old 8, by the Cathedral."

"Oh, I didn't know that," I said.

"Yeah, the government, they pay it. I don't have much in my apartment, though—no TV—so I guess that's why I like to walk around."

"Alright, well have a good day, Bruce," said Sean.

Sock and I each said Bye. We walked inside. I looked out the window. Bruce was walking away. He took really short but quick steps, and he kept his shoulders above his neck.

"That guy is fucking crazy," said Sean.

———————

My senior year of high school I finally went to a dance again. I hadn't gone to one since middle school. I had always said I disliked dances, but I had always wanted to go to a school dance, but I had never wanted to risk asking someone.

I asked Kaitlyn Franco before Spanish class. She was in her seat, behind my seat. I smiled and said hello and sat down. I turned to her.

"Hey," I said. "Do you want to go to Homecoming with me?"

"Hey," she said. She looked behind me.

"Sure," she said. "That'd be great."

"Cool," I said. "It should be fun."

We went with a group of friends to a fancy restaurant in the Valley. Dad gave me money to spend on dinner.

Kait's mom was the school's guidance counselor at our school, so she was going to be there, regardless. I don't think this came to mind as we sat in front of the school taking chugs from a bottle of vodka. We chased it with Powerade. We made out.

Kait hesitated as we started walking through the parking lot towards the cafeteria.

"What's up?" I asked.

"Take a stick of gum," she said. She handed me a stick of gum. She put one in her mouth.

We walked up to the cafeteria doors. Her aunt was standing outside. Kait hugged her.

"I just blew vodka breath all over my aunt," she said.

On the dance floor I didn't really know what to do but it wasn't a big deal. Usually I hated dancing, it made me feel awkward. I kept bobbing my head and grinding on Kait. I hugged Tony. He said I smelled drunk. I felt drunk. I grinded on Kait. She moved away from me a little. I wondered why the word grind had entered the human vocabulary, in that connotation.

We went to a party in the valley afterwards. It was at this girl's house. Her parents were out of town but her grandma was housesitting. Supposedly no boys were allowed over. I hung out with Miguel and some other guys I knew in a parking lot. Supposedly the girl was going to call someone when her grandma went to bed. Then two dozen dudes would enter the basement. It was a fucking huge house but I can't believe we thought there was a way we could hide the fact that there were two dozen boys roaming around in the basement.

We tried.

I have only the vaguest memories of it. It is sad to wonder if some of the most interesting nights in my life are now dead brain cells.

I remember pouring myself a vodka and cranberry juice, except it wasn't cranberry juice, it was more like Kool-Aid.

I remember trying to roll a joint. I remember ripping all the rolling papers. I remember breaking half the cigarettes in a pack as I tried to empty them to fill with weed.

I remember the grandma whispering down the stairs for the girl to come up.

I remember the girl telling us all to stop talking loudly.

I remember the grandma screaming down the stairs at the girl to get all the guys out of the house.

I remember sitting in Miguel's car. I remember puking in the back seat of his car. I remember not letting anyone know I had just puked. I was quiet about it.

I remember my parents calling me and asking if I was okay.

"YES, I AM OKAY," I said.

"Settle down," said Dad. "We were just checking."

"I'M FINE."

"Tom," said Mom. "We heard there was a big car accident on Old 8."

"I SAID I'M FINE."

"What do you think they do?" Dad asked Mom.

"At the sleepovers, with all guys?" she asked.

"Yeah."

"I don't know. I think they just hang out and play games."

I was sitting in a coffee shop staring at a girl sitting a few tables away. I thought, "Should I go up to her and introduce myself?" I thought that she seemed to be involved in her newspaper and that it would be rude to interrupt her. Also, I hadn't the faintest idea what I would do after I introduced myself and was afraid that it might get awkward. I sat there, drinking my coffee and contemplating this for several minutes. Then she got up from her seat, threw her newspaper in the trash bin, and walked out of the coffee shop.

During my whole time staring at her I had felt self-conscious, reserved, and detached all at the same time. I had realized that if I knew someone was staring at me I would feel very uncomfortable. And yet, it is so much easier to look at someone when there isn't a gaze reflected back at you. But then I realized that everybody else in the coffee shop was involved in completely different endeavors than staring. By the time I thought of that, the girl had left the shop, and so I stood up, paid my bill, and went outside, where I lit a cigarette.

I waited for my new co-worker Joe, who was giving me a

ride home from work, which I had gotten off of three hours before, but he had just gotten off, which was why I had hanging around the cafe. He came as I was finishing my cigarette.

In the car we smoked pretty much the whole bag of pot that we had bought during our lunch break, in the grocery store customer bathroom from someone I didn't know but Joe knew and said was "cool."

Joe didn't really have any ideas of things to do and neither did I and this wasn't very surprising, but it would have better to know before we got high.

"Just drive around," I said.

"Where?" he asked.

"Anywhere," I said.

"Nah."

"What?"

"I don't do this, Tommy boy. I don't drive around aimlessly."

"What do you mean? You never just drive?"

"I mean sometimes I do, but not really. No. I never do. Why the fuck would I just drive around?"

"Just for fun, or to relax, or to look at stuff you haven't seen before. Trees and grass and concrete and exploring new streets and areas and stuff."

"You look at fucking concrete? What the fuck?"

"I don't know."

"So what should we do?"

"Just drive."

"Where?"

"Drive towards Ina Lake. It's pretty there."

"Where's there? What is that?"

"It's over on the other side of where I used to live. Drive past old 8 and then it will be easier to get to. But don't drive past my house—my old house, my parents' house—because I don't want my parents to see me, but—" "You think your parents are just sitting outside just waiting for you to drive by stoned so they can look through the tinted windows and see your bloodshot eyes?"

"I don't know. Jeez."

He drove past Old 8 past my parent's house past my parent's neighborhood. It didn't look like anyone was home.

"Do I just keep going on this?" he asked.

"Yeah it'll turn in a few something but it just turns into the same thing. It's still the same thing."

"OK."

I couldn't wait to see what happened with the road. I knew which way it would go, but what if there was something different, or what if there was another car right around the corner, broken and parked, and we ran into it and died. I remembered when I was a kid and I went biking with Dad one time, during the time when he was really into cycling and he went out for at least 10 miles every day, even during the winter. We started biking out together, but then as we neared the corner he started to pull ahead.

I said, "Dad, I don't know if I'll be able to keep up."

And he said, "Tom, it's OK. You can turn around whenever you want. Sorry I have a pace to keep."

"OK," I said, watching him pull away from me.

He turned the corner and a couple minutes later I turned the corner too, but I didn't see him when I turned the corner. A car drove past me really fast and the people inside—a bunch of older boys—yelled things at me that didn't make sense. I began to get scared that maybe they were going to kill me or at least maim me. I thought I was in for a real fucking maiming.

They drove down the road and turned a corner. I realized I didn't know exactly where I was anymore, or how to get back home, aside from retracing my steps. There weren't really blocks in this part of town. It was just these huge chunks of land that had lots of trees and grass and roads, but the roads all turned slowly, usually, or when there were sharp turns they always led to culdesacs. But, there was one turn immediately after you turned, as I just had, and that turn had no sidewalk, on the road I was on, just ditches, but there was sidewalk on the road I would turn onto, if I decided to do that.

Sidewalk almost gave it a higher level of civilization, if that was possible, I thought, as looked up at the sky at an airplane that was flying about the eyesore.

I was staring up there when the group of older guys came back in their car. When they saw me, they started yelling. I jumped into the ditch on the side of the road, which apparently was filled with something wet, while they drove past screaming and laughing. My shoes and ankles were soaked, and the ditch smelled a bit like piss, or poop, or both. I got up, got out, and got on my bike, and turned the corner onto the street with the sidewalk. It led back to a street I recognized that also had sidewalk, which led back to the street that my house was on.

On the day I was driving around with Joe, we didn't turn onto the sidewalked street. We turned on a slow turn that turned into a sharp turn, once you passed a culdesac.

"They call this devil's corner," I said.

"What?"

"They call this devil's corner."

"Are you fucking with me?"

"Yeah, sorry."

"Dumbass."

We drove past some house and we drove past some

woods. I saw a deer. We drove past some houses.

"Stop up here," I told him.

"Why?" he asked.

"There's a good view."

"What?"

"Believe me."

He drove up a little hilly road that had houses and trees on each side.

"Stop here," I said.

He stopped the car and we stared ahead at the Cuyahoga Valley National Park's endless tree tops in the forest below us.

"No, pull up a bit more," I said.

"Maddox," he said, annoyed.

He pulled up a bit more and we could see the tops of the tallest buildings in Akron. There were three or maybe four building peaks that we could see.

"Oh, that's nice," he said.

"Yeah, It's kind of cool," I said.

We stared at the buildings and trees, while the classic rock song—I had heard it probably 100 times but I couldn't remember its name—changed into sounds of screaming, and almost laughing, animals.

"What the fuck," said Joe.

I started laughing.

"What the fuck!" he said in a louder voice.

"What is this shit?" he asked.

"I don't know," I said, laughing.

I felt more stoned than I had felt in a long time. I remembered how when I first smoked pot I wouldn't be able to function, but then eventually I would be able to function again. This felt like that. I felt like I couldn't move, or think, even if I tried really hard. I was physically and mentally paralyzed.

I slowly, painfully turned my eyes to view the surroundings. Houses were to my right and left, outside car windows, the buildings and trees were still in front of me, and I couldn't turn to look around.

"This shit must be laced with something," I said.

We were parked in front of a house, to my left, and a man came out of it. He had a goatee, glasses, balding head, and a belly, and he was wearing a sweater and jeans and boots.

"What the fuck?" I said.

"What the fuck?" said Joe.

The man began walking across his lawn.

"What should I do?" I asked.

"I don't know, let's drive away."

"Okay."

"No. Actually roll down your window."

"Really?"

The man came close to the car and shouted, "Roll down your window," at me.

I rolled it down.

"What are you guys doing?"

Neither of us said anything.

"Are you guys lost?"

"No," I said.

"Then get the hell out of here," he said.

"What?" I said, reflexively.

"You can't just park on the street in front of someone's house," he said.

I was confused. Couldn't you?

"Get out of here," he said, "or I will call the cops."

"Go," I said to Joe, "fucking go."

Joe pushed on the gas but the car was in park and it just made loud revving noises. I looked at the guy but he was just looking at us. Joe started driving. We reached the bottom of the hill, where there was a dead end, and he asked me where to go.

"I don't know," I said. "You choose."

INDIANA JONES #4

"This is the only hydraulic fracturing (or "fracking", as some call it) injection well in Summit County. There are many more in the southern and eastern portions of the state, but we won't be going there, of course. This one is on the land of an individual named Randal Myers, an independent agricultural and industrial contractor, and while he has reported his drinking water is fine, nearby neighbors have indeed reported a murky color, not like water (although not necessarily unlike water). However, New Method Gas, the company with the lease on portions of Myers' land, says that that they believe they have contained the contamination and stopped the spread of the leaks. Preventive measures such as subsurface concrete and metal walls have been used in order to assure that no water is affected, although independent researchers claim that they have been finding evidence to the contrary. The government has contracted one independent environmental research group to investigate but it says their findings will not be concluded and reported until 2018, or seven years from now.

"What is injected into the wells? I have a list of the chemicals here….give me a second….here they are….they are: hydrochloric acid, sodium chloride, polyacrylamide, ethylene glycol, borate salts, sodium carbonates, potassium carbonates, glutaraldehyde guar, tartaric acid, citric acid, red 40, isopropanol, strontium salts, lithium salts, lithium carbonate, calcium chloride, cryolite, barium chloride, copper acetoarsenite, strontium, magnesium powder, acetone, acetic acid, benzene, cadmium hexamine, naphthalene toluene cadmium, hexavalent chromium, polybrominated biphenyls, and polybrominated diphenyl ether.

"So yes, those are the chemicals involved in this particular natural gas process.

"OK, we need to go now. We have a busy day tomorrow. Your last day."

I finally worked up the courage to ask Chelsea on a date, although it was after she had stopped working at BAM, and it was over Facebook. We met at Steak and Shake, a retro burger joint usually frequented by families and groups of teenagers. I went there with groups of friends in high school. It wasn't the most romantic dining spot, but I hadn't even figured I would get the date. I didn't think it was possible to add girls on Facebook, send them a message asking if they wanted to quote end quote hang out, and get them to agree to go on a date. Of course, on some level I must have thought it was possible, because I had tried the tactic several times before, so I guess my surprise was more that that time it actually worked.

I arrived in the parking lot twenty minutes early. I looked inside, realized I was really early, she wasn't there, and pulled back onto the road. Steak and Shake is located near Chapel Hill Mall, so I drove around the different strip mall parking lots and the big parking lot of the main shopping center with a food court and chains of stores. It was pleasant driving around the lots. The lots were much bigger than they needed to be. I didn't know what the hell the planners of the area could have been thinking. There wasn't one section of parking lot that was greater than a quarter full, so I was able to cut through across the parking lines, avoiding the slow drone of cars that still kept their movement within the complexes' authorized, signified paths.

I stopped in the main mall's parking lot and got out to smoke a cigarette. Although I had never asked her I already knew that Chelsea was not a cigarette smoker and would not approve of smoking. As we were going to a movie after lunch, I wanted to make sure I had my nicotine fix because it would be hours before I would have another chance. After I smoked my first one, I smoked another. I counted the number of spaces between my car and the next parked car. There were sixteen empty spaces between us.

I drove back to Steak and Shake. I didn't see her inside but I went in anyways. There didn't seem to be any point in waiting. The server asked if I was dining alone. I said no. She seated me at a booth.

Chelsea arrived about five minutes later. She looked around and I waved. She smiled and walked over to the table.

"Hey!" she said.

"Hey!" I said. I felt my voice rise.

She sat down.

"What's up?" I asked.

"Not a whole lot," she said. "Sorry I'm late."

"Oh, no problem," I said. "I just got here."

"Great!"

"So, yeah, this is Steak and Shake."

"Yeah, this was a great choice," she said. "I love this place."

"Yeah, I used to come here a lot."

"Sorry again I was late. I was busy helping my mom pack up some boxes to put in storage, and I completely lost track of time."

"Oh, no problem."

She smiled. I smiled, looked at my menu. A gnawing sensation began to creep up my back into my neck. I wondered what the hell I was doing. I had never said more than five or six words to her at a time, and yet here I was trying to be casual like we were old friends.

"I must admit," she said. "I was a little surprised when I saw your Facebook message."

"Oh," I said. "Why?"

"Oh, I don't know," she said. "It's just we never really talked much at BAM."

"Right," I said.

She smiled at me. I could sense she wanted me to say more.

"I mean, I don't know," I said. "I just always wanted to get around to knowing you when we worked there, and I never got the chance."

The memories of the hundreds of times she had come over during the end of store hours to get my register began to flood towards the front of my brain. My eyes bulged.

"No, that's great," she said. "I was glad you messaged me. This will be fun."

"Cool. Yeah, we get to know each other now, at least."

"Exactly."

I closed my menu. I began biting a nail. I stopped biting it and locked my hands together in my lap and started twiddling my thumbs.

"So what's your job now?" I asked.

"I work at First Savings Bank," she said, "As a teller at the counter."

"Nice," I said.

"Yeah, I like it a lot."

"I'm guessing it pays more than BAM?" I asked.

"Yeah, it pays pretty well," she said.

"Is that why you quit?"

"Yeah, plus I was going away to Disney."

"Oh, yeah. I forgot that you went down there. That was through Akron U., right?"

"Yeah, Disney has a nice exchange program."

"What did you do exactly?"

"Oh, I worked in the park. I worked at the Helium Drop ride."

"Cool," I said, even though it sounded really boring.

"Yeah, I also was working an internship at Epcot too."

"What was that like?"

"It was—"

A waitress came over to our table as Chelsea was in the middle of her sentence. I was relieved.

"Hello, I'm Dianne," said the waitress. "How are you guys today?"

Dianne had dyed black hair and wore a lot of make-up. She probably fit with the ex-goth, burnout crowd that held most of the positions at the restaurant.

"Good," said Chelsea.

"Yeah, good," I said.

"Do you guys know what you want yet, or would you like some more time?"

"I'm ready," I said.

"Yeah, I'm ready."

"Okay, go ahead whenever you're ready," said the waitress.

I looked at Chelsea. She looked at me and then she looked at the waitress and then she looked at her menu.

"I will have the small chili," said Chelsea.

"Alright. Anything to drink?"

"A Coke, I guess."

"We only have Pepsi."

"That's fine. Diet Pepsi, though?"

I looked at Dianne. She wrote down Chelsea's order on her pad. She looked at me.

"I will have the steakburger," I said.

"Alright. Anything to drink?"

"I will have a banana spilt milkshake. And water, please."

"I'd like a water as well," said Chelsea.

"Alright," said Dianne. "I will be right back with your drinks and waters."

We told her thanks. She walked back to the kitchen. I noticed a guy I had gone to grade school with was working in the kitchen. I thought his name was Tyler but I couldn't remember.

"What were we talking about?" asked Chelsea.

"Your semester in Disney."

"Oh yeah," she said. "It was good."

"So you're glad you left BAM, then?"

"Oh, by the time I got back from Disney I felt that I was done with BAM. It felt like that part of my life had passed kind of sort of."

"That makes sense. I can't wait to leave BAM."

"Oh, I still miss it sometimes, but I just wanted to move on. It was a great place to work, though."

I nodded until I realized she was the first person I had ever heard say that.

"Oh," I said, "I mean, it's fine for what it is."

"Exactly," she said.

I looked around the room. There was a group of teenagers sitting at one table. Families were at a couple tables. At the booth diagonal in front of us there was a couple that looked to be on a date. They looked much more comfortable and much less animated.

"So, you're at Kent right now, right?" she asked.

"Yep," I said. "I live at home with my parents and I took classes there the past two semesters, and probably this summer too. I am hoping to go back down to Athens this fall, though."

"Oh," she said. "That's where you started out at, right?"

"Yeah, I went there my first year," I said.

"Why'd you leave?"

"Oh, I don't know. I was having some problems, mentally. Academically I was fine. But yeah, I don't know, I got into drugs and just was pretty crazy. All over that now, though."

She smiled mechanical.

"How long do you have left?"

"Well, I am going into my third year at Akron, but all my credits from the semester at Disney didn't go through. Plus, I changed my major."

"From what? To what?"

"Advertising and psychology to International Business Accounting."

"Cool. You want to live outside the U.S. eventually?"

"Maybe," she said. "We'll see. I also have always wanted to live in New York City. Manhattan."

"I saw on your Facebook that you visited there a couple weeks ago."

"Yeah! It was great."

"Yeah, I went once in high school and then I went once earlier this year. It's great. I think I might move there after I graduate."

"Really? Yeah, it would be amazing. But who knows… it's so expensive."

"Yep. It is."

I looked around for our waitress.

"I wonder where she is," I said. "She never came back with our drinks."

"Yeah, I don't know," said Chelsea.

"I think I might know one of the guys that works here," I said.

"Oh yeah," she said, looking around.

"Where'd you go to high school?" I asked.

"L.A.C.V."

"Ah, the Lord's Academy of Cuyahoga Valley."

"Yep. That's what it stands for."

I looked around the restaurant again. Where the fuck was our waitress?

"Where'd you go?"

"I went to Falls," I said. "It was free, obviously."

"Yeah, that's funny," she said.

"Yeah, it was okay. Right down the street from where you live, right?"

"Yep."

"Do you remember when someone vandalized the outside walls of your school?" I asked.

"I don't think so."

"It was when I was a junior, and you graduated the same year, right?"

"2005?"

"Yeah. So when we were juniors."

"What was it?" she asked.

"Oh, I remember exactly," I said. "I think it was a bunch of big penises with spray paint. I know on Loyola they also wrote: Lesbians Rule, or something."

"That's horrible," she said.

"Yeah," I said, even though I had thought it was kind of funny.

Our waitress came over.

"Small chili?"

Chelsea held up a hand.

"Steak burger deluxe?"

I held up a hand.

"Oh you guys never got your drinks?"

"No," I said.

"I'll be right back with those."

She came back with our drinks.

"Sorry about that. Enjoy."

I was glad that we could just eat. I wondered if we would make out at the movie.

"Is your chili good?" I asked.

"It's great," she said. "How about your burger and shake?"

"Yeah, they're good."

My steak burger was not as good as I remembered it being when I was in high school. I ate it though, because I was hungry and I hadn't eaten breakfast. I looked outside. It was the beginning of summer. It looked like it was going to rain, though.

After we finished, I waved down the waitress. She took forever to come over. I asked for the check. She took forever to come back with the check.

I picked up the check and got out my wallet. The bill was 12.15. I got out a twenty.

"Oh, thanks," said Chelsea.

"No problem," I said. "We are on a date, right?"

"I guess," she said, "But we never really clarified."

"Well, now it's clarified."

I went up to the register and handed the cashier the twenty. Once I had my change we walked outside.

"I guess I'll meet you at the theatre?" I said.

"Yeah," she said, "Sounds good."

I got into my car. I really wanted to smoke a cigarette as I drove to the theatre a few blocks away, but I didn't want her to smell it. I decided not to smoke one.

We were watching the new Indiana Jones movie. There

hadn't been an Indiana Jones movie that I had seen in the theatre before. It was stadium seating and we sat in the front of the bleachers on the right.

The movie was bad. Harrison Ford was too old. It didn't seem to make sense for him to be jumping onto running horses and carriages. The plot was bad. Only the first movie had a really good plot.

I looked at her and she was staring at the screen. I put my arm around her. She fidgeted a little. I looked at her again.

"Hey," she said. She leaned back towards me.

I rubbed my hand back and forth across a spot on her back for a while. My hand slid behind her back. It fell asleep. I moved it up. She fidgeted and looked at me.

"Sorry," I said, "Just repositioning myself."

The movie was almost over. I don't remember how it ended.

We walked outside and it was cloudier but still light out. We had parked next to each other. There were only a couple dozen cars in the lot. Tuesday matinees weren't popular.

"Well, we should do this again," I said.

"Yeah," she said, "We should."

We got in our cars. I smoked a cigarette on the way home. I didn't feel anything.

I knew after the date that I wasn't that into her, but I still figured it couldn't hurt to put in a little effort, so I sent her a couple text messages after a week or two. She responded the second time. We eventually agreed to meet at Starbucks for coffee. I had suggested lunch or mini golf. I had no idea why I suggested mini golf. It was almost like I deliberately kept suggesting lame high school activities. She suggested coffee after each suggestion, so we got coffee.

I got there before her. My throat had been hurting lately.

I had been having trouble breathing. I smoked a cigarette on the way there, anyways. I waited in my car until she showed up ten minutes later. I cleared my throat. I could feel mucus clogging my lungs.

"Hey," I said.

"Hey," she said.

I went in for a hug and she accepted it. We went inside. It was a nice June day, and clouds were puffy and white. She ordered a cappuccino and I ordered an iced coffee. We sat at a table outside.

"So how's everything been going?" I asked.

"Good," she said. "How have you been?"

"I'm good. Just been busy with work a lot."

"Yeah, me too. Are you getting ready to go back to Athens? To OU?"

"I mean, that's the plan, for the end of the summer. I don't really have to do anything, though, like beforehand."

"You like college, though?" she asked.

"Yeah, I mean. I like it."

"That's good. I am not looking forward to school starting back again here in a few weeks."

"Oh, are you taking summer classes?" I asked.

"Yeah. Are you?"

"No, but I'm gonna go to some at Kent this summer."

"Cool."

"Yeah, kind of busy," I said. "I'd like to meet up again, though."

"Yeah, see, that's kind of something I wanted to talk about."

"What?"

"I don't know if we should date anymore," she said.

"We've been on two dates now," I said.

"Yeah, I know."

"What's the problem?"

"I mean, it's the long distance thing. See, when we first met up I didn't realize that you were going to be heading back to Athens this fall. I thought you were going to be living around here for a while."

"Oh."

"But then we met and it was nice, so I didn't know what to do. I like you."

"Yeah.

"It's just the long distance thing."

"Okay."

"Is that okay?"

"Yeah, that's fine," I said.

"Really?" she asked.

"Yeah, we can still be friends anyways, right?" I asked. The words seemed void.

She nodded and said, "Yeah, of course."

I took a large sip from my iced coffee. We sat silent for a few minutes. There was another couple sitting out there. The patio was only fifteen or twenty feet on each side. I looked at the girl. The guy had his back turned to me. She locked eyes with me before looking away. I figured she might have heard Chelsea and me talking.

"Well, I need to go runs some errands for my mom," said Chelsea.

I looked up. She hadn't been daydreaming.

"Oh, okay," I said.

"Are you okay?" she asked.

"Yeah, I just lost my train of thought," I said.

"Oh."

"We should meet up again sometime," I said.

"Yeah."

"Just as friends."

"Yeah, of course. I'd love that."

She seemed to be done with her cappuccino. I finished my iced coffee. We got up.

"See you later," I said, as I walked to my car.

"Bye, Tom," she said.

I got in my car and lit a cigarette. She waved out her window as she drove by, but her fake smile died when she saw my face with a cigarette in it.

On the drive home I began coughing repeatedly, uncontrollably. I wondered if I was having an asthma attack. I hadn't had an asthma attack since I was seven. I threw my cigarette out the window.

I pulled by the curb outside the house because mom and dad's cars were both in the driveway. I walked inside. Mom was making a grocery list on the kitchen table.

"Hey, Tom," she said.

"Hey," I said.

"How was your date?"

"Good," I said, as I walked into the kitchen to pour myself a glass of water.

"How was your friend?"

"She was good," I said. "We're both busy so we don't get to meet up much."

I finished the glass of water. I poured myself another one and went upstairs. The sun was beating down in my room so I pulled down the shade. It was pretty dark but I didn't feel like turning on the bedside lamp.

I didn't see Chelsea again for almost a year. I went back to school in Athens. She still lived with her mom. When I was home for spring break the next year I ran into her at the bank. The location she worked at wasn't the closest to the house, but I was in the area.

She was surprised to see me. I smiled.

"Hey, do you use this bank?" she asked.

"Yeah, this is my bank," I said.

"Cool. How are you?"

"I'm good."

"You?"

"Yeah, good. Do you like being back in Athens."

"It's alright. Yeah, I like it."

"Cool."

"I actually had remembered you worked here, so I decided to stop by."

"Oh, that's nice."

"Yeah. I was wondering if maybe you want to hang out sometime?"

"Yeah, sure. What'd you have in mind?"

"I don't know. I was just thinking of taking you out. Maybe to dinner or something. See a movie."

"Yeah, that sounds great," she said.

We went to a dinner and a movie the next night. We went to a Mexican restaurant that wasn't Taco Bell. It had a new name every time I was home. My parents used to take me there sometimes when I was a teenager. The only spike in conversation was when I told her I liked her sweater. It was a nice sweater. It was black and had a folded ringed collar. Her breasts were noticeable because it wasn't too baggy.

"Thanks," she said. "Your shirt is nice too."

I found that remark horribly lame. She didn't even offer an original compliment. She just rephrased my compliment and added the word too.

She went to the bathroom after she finished her plate. The waiter came by and I got the check.

We saw a spoof film. I realized how spoof films were

becoming retarded. They didn't make any sense at all anymore. Most spoof movies just spoofed everything they could think of from the pop culture of the past few years, and sometimes it seemed liked just spoofs of spoofs, with seemingly endless levels of spoof. Maybe that's what spoof movies do. I didn't understand.

We sat in the back of the bleachers. I put my arm around her. The same routine from our first date. This time I went in to kiss her. I tried for just a peck on the forehead, because she was shorter than me. She moved her head when she felt my beard. I looked back at the screen. I tried to kiss her again. She moved away again.

"No," she said.

"Sorry," I said. I frowned.

"I'm not like that," she said.

"Like what?"

"Like that."

I was sitting in my car, tired, on my way home from the doctor. I was only five minutes from home when I hit a traffic jam right by that bridge.

People were screaming at something. I got out of my car to see what was happening.

There was a guy standing on the edge of the bridge, looking over into the valley below.

People were screaming, "Jump!" and "Get it over with, asshole!" and things like that.

Some cops were running up from the opposite end of the bridge. They couldn't get their cop cars close enough because of the jam so they had to walk. That probably meant that the guy had been up there for a while, because the jam was already pretty big. The cops must not have found it urgent. Lots of people jumped off that bridge.

I sat watching the cops talk to the man. I wondered what they could say. Here was a guy who was obviously ready to jump. And there's a bunch of people telling him to jump. The only people telling him not to jump were a couple cops, whose job it was to enforce the law, and the law said that suicide was illegal. Why would he trust them?

I don't know why he did but he did. They got him down and took him away. People got really silent after he got down.

A few years later, the federal government wrote our state a big check for economic stimulus. One of the spending choices the state government made was to build a big fence on the sides of that bridge. They said it was to reduce the trash that people were throwing off it.

I got my hair cut at 4:00 PM on Wednesday afternoons, every three weeks. My barber, Irene, marked me down for the entire year every third week. The schedule changed during holidays, but there was a system in place, so that every third week it would still be cut.

I remember I really wanted to get my hair cut that Wednesday. I didn't want to look like a scrub (the word for the dudes who wore the same clothes most days and didn't have good hygiene; the corresponding term for females was "pigeons"). The school bells let out and I was the first of the kids from my neighborhood to leave the building, so I began slowly walking towards the street to cross because I didn't like waiting around. Some days Dad would drive home on that road, out of his way, just to make sure that I wasn't straying from that road. They had their reasons. I had gotten into some fights with my friends. Also, the other road that I would usually walk home on was Old 8, where businesses got robbed sometimes and a few homeless wandered around sometimes.

That day a couple friends and I decided to head towards Old 8, instead of taking Huron Boulevard. A man who owned a house on the corner of Phelps and Huron had yelled at us the day before because we walked on his lawn. Most days he would be out mowing it, watering it, or trimming the areas around the sidewalk and devil's strip. He had white hair and wore wide, dark-rimmed glasses and a wife beater. We would come upon his lawn walking three-, four-, or five-file and he would scream at us. School kids left to their own rule do not generally walk in formation. We could have walked on the other side of the road, but that would have taken us ever so slightly astray from the most direct passage back to our neighborhood, which is what w did that day. We cut across Portage Trail through some back streets and made our way to the comic book and laser disc stores. Only one of us actually read comics, which the rest of us considered dorky. We usually looked at the Pokemon and Magic Cards. I was most interested in the laser disk store, Time Traveler, which no longer sold laser discs but it still had a large sign on it saying LASER DISK. I also enjoyed the Star Wars action figures that were for sale in the comic book store. I had strict guidelines set for myself over the purchase of CDs or action figures. I would save up half of my 10 dollars that I was given for lunch money each week (not much, but mom also packed me a lunch because she knew of the diseases growing in that cafeteria) and spend that money on either : a.) an action figure costing less than $10, or b:) a compact disc costing less than $10.

I looked at the action figures behind the cashier's counter and walked away. I could only afford the ones that were on the shelf in the aisle with the action figures, but I didn't want Lando Calrissian from the Tatooine scene in Return of the Jedi. It was 7.99 and I could afford it. I wanted the Yoda from The Empire Strikes Back that was behind the cashier's counter. But it cost $20.00. I asked the clerk how much it was and he said 20 dollars. I wanted it, but I couldn't have it. We left.

When I got home, Dad's car was already in the driveway. I said goodbye to my friends. They were going to play basketball but I would need to get permission first.

"Where were you?" Dad asked.

"What do you mean?" I asked.

"It's 3:50, we were supposed to go get your haircut."

"Oh, I forgot."

"It's not nice to make Irene wait. You're the one who has been asking if you could go get it cut. I thought maybe you could have lasted another week this time."

"Irene always puts me down for every three weeks, though."

"She wouldn't mind changing it, Tom. And, come to think of it, she's worried about you, too, like the rest of us. You don't talk anymore. You're not as friendly as you used to be."

"Ok. I don't know. I don't like it when it gets long. It gets greasy."

"How are you doing in your classes?"

"Fine."

"You sure?"

"Yeah. They're going pretty good."

"Well, I got a midterm report from your school today."
"Really?"
"Yes."
"So?"
"So you have 3 C's and a B."
"Really?"
"You must have known this already, Tom. From tests and quizzes and homework. They give you grades."
"I, um."
"So you lied?"
"No."
"Yes you did."
"I, um. I will make the grades up during the second half of the semester," I said.
"Tom, even if you get A's for the rest of the time, you'll still end up with B's."
"What do you want me to say?"
"Excuse me?"
"What do you want me to say? Can we just go to the barber?"
"Your hair doesn't really matter to me at this point."
"What?"
"We're talking about grades."
"But I thought we shouldn't make Irene wait?"
"What are you going to do about these grades, Tom?"
"I DON'T KNOW. I DON'T CARE."
His eyes widened. I had never really yelled back at my parents since I had been a little kid.
I started screaming, "AHHHHH." I started running through the kitchen and the game room and the living room and then back into the solarium.
"Goddammit," he yelled.
I turned as I got to the doorway. I put up my fists. His

eyes got wide again.

"Oh, is that what you want?" he said. "Do you want to fight?"

I looked at him. I was two inches taller than him, and still growing.

"NO. FUCKING GOD."

I ran outside. Snow was falling on the ground. I realized October was almost over. I put my head in the grass next to the driveway. The snow was sticking.

Dad came out of the house. He told me to get in the car. I got in the car. His face was red. We drove up the hill, he turned right onto Old 8, and we made our way to the barber.

I got my haircut. Afterwards, he got his neck shaved. I sat in a short chair next to the rotatable barber chair he now occupied. As I looked through the latest issue of Sports Illustrated For Kids, she whispered to him. I think she asked if it had gotten any better. His response was hushed, but I think he said, "No, it's actually gotten worse." I knew they were talking about me.

The following spring, I rode with him to the horticulture nursery on the outskirts of town. When I had gotten into the car I noticed there was a knife on the dashboard. It looked rusty but sharp. I wondered if he was going to kill me. I was still a trouble, but I didn't think I had become that much of a trouble. We talked about the Little League team I had recently joined. I kept glancing at the knife, and the conversation was delayed a couple times as I forgot what we were talking about.

We got to the nursery. He talked with the owner about plants and her kids. They were grown ups, but he had taught her son as a freshman in college at one point. I wandered around the store, looking at different items.

COME BACK WHENEVER

•

"Okay, is everyone seated? Okay. This has been a great trip—one of the best I remember. I don't know if you have all got as much out of this as you hoped you would, but it has been fun to be with all of you. Talking with all of you has truly been a pleasure. I have enjoyed talking to you.

"I think that we can all agree that there is something at work here. This area is at a crossroads. It may not be important. I just want to thank you all for allowing me to do this."

"Did you have a good trip, Dave?"

"Yeah, I have enjoyed this myself. I have to thank you for driving. Without someone to navigate through this I would just be an asshole sitting up in my seat backwards in the way I told them not to sit in their seats."

"These folks are pretty interesting, no?"

"No thoughts? I can't blame you."

"Alright, all. I wanted this trip to be meaningful for all of you. I wanted to say lessons, but I don't want to preach, or teach. But I hope all of you have seen what I am talking about. The eyesore. Cedar Point. The Cuyahoga.

"Now, I am not saying this is a metaphor. I am saying this is real. We are going to be going to the airport the terrorists flew out of, and we are going to be returning to where they were headed.

"I think we have 15 or 20 minutes left before we are back."

"I don't even like getting political, but I feel that's the only way they might listen."

"Do you care?"

"Oh well, who does anyways? I don't."

"We are coming up on the airport, all. Please buckle up, because we will be making turns as we are getting off the highway. We will have two hours at the airport. I don't expect there will be too much of a crowd at the airport, but I still have to ask that you stay within my vicinity, and that we all stay together."

―――――――

I was leaving Ohio the next day to return to New York. Aside from the one night with Sock, I hadn't seen anyone I knew besides my parents. I texted Laura and asked if she wanted to go for a bite and a movie. She said okay.

"I'm going out to the movies with Laura," I told Mom.

"Oh?" she said. "That's nice."

"Yeah."

"What movie are you going to go see?"

"I think we are going to see The Man Who Shot Liberty Valance."

"The Jimmy Stewart movie?"

"No it's a remake of it."

"Oh, that sounds good."

"Yeah."

"What are you guys talking about?" asked Dad, as he walked into the kitchen.

"Oh, I'm going to see a movie with Laura," I said.

"That sounds fun. What movie?"

"The Man Who Shot Liberty Valance."

"The John Wayne movie?"

"No, it's a remake."

"Oh well, tell me how it is."

"I will," I said. I sat down in the solarium and began tying my shoes.

"Be careful driving," he said. "The roads are slippery."
"I will."
"Tell Laura we said hi."
"Okay."
"Have a good time," said Mom.
"Alright. Bye."

I walked out to the driveway and started Mom's car. I hadn't seen Laura since the night we slept together in New York. I rolled up the hill towards Old 8.

Laura grew up on 11th Street and Portage Trail. Her parents still live there but she lives in Kent, a few dozen miles west. She was staying at home with her parents that week, though.

"I just kind of miss being at home," she said, as we drove to the mall.

"But you only live half an hour away," I said.

"I know," she said, "I just get tired of roommates and the same old room. It's nice to come home."

"That's true," I said. "It is nice to come home."

I said I wasn't hungry but she said she kind of was. We went to a place called Panera. They serve soup and salads and sandwiches and bagels and pastries. I got clam chowder in a sourdough bowl.

"What'd you get?" I asked her.

"The tomato and cheese panini."

"Ah."

We waited for our food. They gave us each those annoying buzzers that light up when your food is ready. I don't know why they had to use such complicated means to get people their food. I don't know what happened to the good old calling out receipt numbers. It seemed pretentious.

"That looks good," I told her, when we had sat down and started eating.

"Yeah it is," she said. "You want to try some?"

"No, I'm fine."

"You sure?"

"Yeah, I'm not too hungry."

We finished our meals. I went up and bought a coffee.

"Do you think I can take this into the movie?" I asked.

"Yeah," she said.

"How?"

"Just don't drink it in front of the cashier at the theatre."

"You think so?"

"I don't know why that wouldn't work."

"Okay," I said.

I was able to get the coffee in. The movie starred Ryan Gosling and Matt Damon. It was a pretty good movie.

I looked at her at one point. I realized I wasn't attracted to her. I wasn't sure if it was because we had only been seeing each other so fleetingly or if it was because something else had changed. I didn't know what that something else would even be, though.

I drove her home afterwards. I said the parts I didn't like. She said the parts she liked. I said the parts I liked.

When we pulled into her parents' driveway, I leaned over and hugged her. She embraced me for a few seconds. She wished me well. We agreed we would meet the next time I was home.

I watched her walk into her parents'. I pulled out of the driveway. I remembered how I had been so into her so briefly that one night back in New York, but I didn't really remember it.

———————

On the drive to the airport I was looking at a field on one side of the road when I remembered a recurring daydream from my childhood. When I was maybe nine or ten, I would be driving around with Mom, or I would be walking around the house when no one else was home, and I would have these thoughts that were like nightmares, except that they weren't at night and I wasn't asleep—they were daydreams. I would imagine my sister and Dad being dead. They died in a car accident, I think was my daydream. I don't know why it was them, but it was. The rest of us had this sadness, this emptiness, this heavy emptiness that couldn't be described. I would think about how we were carrying on, and I would imagine soft, slow, sad tunes always playing in the background. I never could figure out why I had started thinking those things, but after a while I stopped thinking that and was able to forget pretty easily, without much thought, that I ever had, though I still remembered sometimes, as we drove around in cars, which as I drove them less and less just seemed like lottery balls in a death machine.

"I think I'm on the aisle."

"Oh, well my ticket says the aisle, too."

"I don't know what to tell you."

I moved over to the middle seat. A man was reading a pamphlet next to me. It wasn't a flight safety brochure. It was old and it was written in a different language. There was a group of what looked like college students in the back of the plane. They all had fancy clothes on. I wondered if they were from New York or Ohio. I couldn't see much out the window. I didn't have much legroom.

The flight took twenty minutes to take off. When we got into the air I heard an explosion. It sounded like it came from the plane. It shook around a bit and then it went back down to the ground.

All the passengers were talking to each other. I made a confused face to the man who had taken the aisle seat.

"Ladies and gentleman," said the pilot over the intercom. "We have experienced a malfunction. I don't know what it is yet. I have to ask that you sit tight until we resolve this issue."

A few minutes later he came back on: "Ladies and gentleman, sorry for this inconvenience. We believe it was a problem in the engine. It looks like they are going to keep us here for a bit while they figure this out."

I looked out the window. There were fire trucks driving up.

After twenty minutes the fire trucks drove away.

"We are now going to be returning to the gate. At that point, we will be leaving this aircraft and boarding another. Once again, I am sorry for this inconvenience."

"It was my prayers," said the guy by the window. He held up his prayer book. "I said them right before we left," he said.

"Oh," I said.

I took a flight safety brochure out of the seat in front of me. It wasn't a bad read.

The plane lands at LaGuardia three and a half hours after it was supposed to. I walk outside and wait for a bus. It comes twenty or so minutes later. I take the bus over the bridge and across Harlem. I get off the bus at 116th and Broadway. I walk across the street and down the stairs to the subway platform. There are a couple homeless guys sitting on a bench across the tracks. A downtown train comes, stops, and they are still sitting there when it leaves. Probably some cop will come kick them out eventually and they will get on the train. They will ride it to the end of the line and try to go back to sleep. I can't imagine. I remember sitting in Grand Central once. It was the middle of the day. I was in the cafeteria on the bottom floor, right outside the Oyster Bar. I sat at a table eating some okay pizza that cost five dollars a slice. There was a homeless guy passed out at the table next to mine. A cop came by and nudged him with his billy club. The homeless guy stirred. He opened up a newspaper that was on the table next to him. I don't really know how I feel about cops or homeless people. I guess I just feel bad for both in different ways.

 The train comes ten or fifteen minutes later. I take it two stops and get off. I am sitting in my apartment in my room staring at my computer. I check my Gmail. I realize my Gmail background is stupid. I have had it for a year, maybe more. It's not good. I click on Account Settings. I click on some of the background options. After some heavy deliberation I decide on the plainest one, the basic HTML one, the original Gmail background. I check Facebook. I see a status update from one of my high school classmates. Her photos are all privatized. If I had a yearbook I could look at her face. That would help me remember what she looked like. I can't really remember. My yearbook is under my bed back in Ohio. When I was in high school, my parents finally decided to get Internet during my final year. I was only allowed to use the Internet for an hour a day. They felt this was very lenient. It probably was. During the rest of my weekday evenings I would sit in my room. I would write in my journal. I would write some poems, but mostly lists. The rest of the time I would read books. When I started to lose interest in the novel I was reading I would get the yearbooks out from under my bed. I would stare at people. I didn't know most of them.

Andrew Duncan Worthington is the author of the poetry e-book HOT DOGS! and founding editor of *Keep This Bag Away From Children*. His work has been published by Vice, Bookslut, Mr. Beller's Neighborhood, 3:AM Magazine, and Everyday Genius, among others. He teaches English and special education in New York City. Find him at: andrewduncanworthington.com.

CPSIA information can be obtained
at www.ICGtesting.com
Printed in the USA
FFOW03n1238170315
11799FF